everything
i need

everything
i need

AN 'I FOUND YOU SERIES' NOVEL

K.B. BARRETT

everything
i need

Inquiries: kbbarrettauthor@gmail.com

ISBN: 9798713730376

Second Edition JUNE 2021

10 9 8 7 6 5 4 3 2

ALSO BY K.B. BARRETT

'I FOUND YOU SERIES' NOVELS

Everything I Need

Anything For You

Nothing Without You

Something About You

'MOUNTIAN ROADS' NOVELS

Saved by the Mountain Man (prequel)

The Twisted Roads Home

What Drives Us Home

Dedication

I would like to dedicate this book to my late grandmother, who was always my biggest champion. She pushed me to be the best version of myself, and never gave up on me. She taught me that no matter what happens, to remain true to who you are.

I miss you every day.

This one is for you Grandma.

everything i need

I started this journey almost five years ago.

Since then, Everything I Need has transformed into something more than I ever thought possible.

It has been a rollercoaster of a ride. But the support from other Indie authors, my husband, and my friends has been overwhelming, and I wouldn't trade it for anything.

So here is Everything I Need.

I hope you enjoy it as much as I did writing it.

Alice Beckman was no quitter.

She stood in her bathroom, looked in the mirror and told herself that she could do this even though she hated working at the restaurant. In all reality, she didn't really have a choice. Not if she wanted to keep a roof over her head and food in the cupboard. Even if the little rundown one-room apartment was on the wrong side of town and her kitchen didn't hold much beyond top ramen and discounted cans of beans, it was hers. She sighed, still not wanting to leave for work.

About a year ago, her friend Taby had gotten her a job at the restaurant. At first, it had been wonderful. Almost too good to be true. She had been looking for something that would help supplement the trust her parents had left her, but she hadn't been able to find anywhere that would be willing to work around her hours at the local college. She had been getting desperate, worried that her trust money would disappear so quickly that she wouldn't be able to finish school.

She knew that to someone else looking at the situation, her school seemed like a waste of money. But it was what her parents would have wanted, and she was going to make them proud even if it ran her ragged. However, there hadn't been that much to start with. Just enough for a few semesters. It had all worked out, though, when fate had stepped in and Taby had saved her. Not only was it a decent paying job, but she also had the tips at the end of the night. She should have known that it wouldn't last.

Everything changed when the owner decided to sell the restaurant three months ago. At first, she and Taby hadn't been worried about their jobs; they were all told that the contract included an agreement to keep on all the old employees. Then the new management brought a whole staff of new people with them and started to edge people out. They didn't outright fire anybody, but they left them with no choice but to quit. All that remained now were Taby, Bobby the dishwasher, and herself.

She knew that her days working there were numbered; she wouldn't be able to take it much longer. A week in and the new manager had cornered her, propositioning her. She had been horrified and not knowing what else to do, she ran. He turned mean and cruel after that. And things were only getting worse. But until she could find a new job, she was stuck.

She was also tired. One of the new waitresses, Sara, was often out the door before any of the clean-up was done, leaving Alice to do it all. She was barely making her classes in the morning, too tired to get up let alone have time for her homework at night.

It was exhausting.

It was terrible.

It was almost enough to make her cry. Then she would tell herself to buck up. She had applications out everywhere, and she would find something soon. She just had to wait a little longer.

So, there she stood, staring at herself in the cracked mirror, wishing that her mom was there to give her the advice she desperately needed. She often found herself wishing they were still here. Backing her up. It didn't help that every time she looked in the mirror, she saw her mom. Long wavy brown hair, so thick that it was difficult to deal with sometimes. Brown eyes and an average body.

She tried to remind herself that wishers didn't really get anywhere, that only people who got up and worked for it got what they needed. That was what her dad used to say anyways, and she needed to face reality. And the reality was that she was going to miss the bus to work. Grabbing her coat and her bag, with a book to keep her busy, and slipping on her work shoes, she stepped out into the cool evening.

***

"Order up!" The sounds from the kitchen and of dishes clanking were a constant in the busy rush hour, with food being made and waiters running plates to tables. Even Old Bobby was busy, washing and rinsing dishes in more of a hurry than normal.

She, however, was given the quiet, rarely used back banquet room as her section of tables. Something that had become a regular occurrence with the new management, leaving her open to do all the menial tasks like stocking and cleaning the bathrooms. The jobs that nobody else wanted. She figured that the new manager, Boris, had done it on purpose. That if an actual party came to use the room, she most likely wouldn't actually get to wait on the tables.

Being left to the menial jobs didn't mean that she was safe from him though.

One time, when she had been cleaning the extra chairs in the storage room, Boris had come bursting in, his voice loud enough that she knew some of the customers had heard in the main room.

"You clumsy fool! How could you drop all those plates!" His bald head had been glistening with sweat and his eyes held a gleam of untold hatred. He always looked slightly unkempt, his clothes askew and wrinkled.

It always put her off because the restaurant was higher end. They served a rich clientele. He never really was around the customers, though, mostly staying in the kitchen.

It didn't matter what she thought. He was the boss until she found something else. So when he had accused her of breaking the plates, all she could do was take her punishment. Which meant that her next paycheck was going to take a hit.

After talking with Taby, Alice was still nervous about his reaction, especially after Taby had told her about what she had heard. She had said that the new management and owners were rumored to have ties to the local crime family. Taby was always gossiping and normally Alice didn't put much stock into it, but this time she hadn't been able to push it aside.

As time went on, she began to see a difference in how he was treated by some of the customers. It just confirmed her suspicions that Taby was right. People were not really scared of Boris, but they went out of their way to make him happy. To never tell him no. Even if he was sloppy and unkempt.

It made her wonder if they were reacting that way to him or who he worked for. Either way Boris, being who he was, used it to his advantage.

Like the episode with the plates. He had to have known that she had been nowhere near those plates, and now her next paycheck was going to be a whole lot smaller. She wanted to cry at the frustration of it all but hadn't done anything against it.

People always thought it was one of her biggest downfalls and Taby was constantly trying to get her to be more confrontational.

What Taby didn't get was that she didn't have a choice. Making sure her parents' dream came true was more important than anything else.

Standing up to Boris just wasn't an option.

Chapter 2

"I'm going on break. Watch my tables, and don't you dare try to take some of my tips, you thief. You got me?" Sara sneered, leaning down to get in her face. She was down on her knees scrubbing the bathroom floors, as the mop had suspiciously disappeared a while ago.

"Yes, Sara."

She barely resisted rolling her eyes. She was technically a waitress and could handle the tables just fine, but Sara treated her as if she couldn't do anything. It'd been tough for the last couple of months because she hadn't been able to bring home any extra tips. Hence the top ramen in her cupboard. She wanted nothing more than to say something back but knew that Sara wouldn't hesitate to tell Boris, and then her job could be yanked out from under her.

Shaking her head at her situation, she walked out and started checking tables, refilling drinks, and putting out the orders that were waiting on her. It almost was nice to be back out here, she thought. Some of the jobs that Boris had her doing were awful, and she really missed waiting on the tables.

She was picking up a plate and double-checking everything when Taby came up behind her and started preparing her table's order.

"You okay?" Taby whispered to her.

"Yes," she whispered back and gave her a quick smile to reassure her, then looked away quickly when she heard the door open. She knew that Taby worried about her. She was constantly trying to tell her that she needed to just quit. A little hypocritical of her. But she also knew that Boris basically ignored Taby, so it wasn't as bad for Taby as it was for her. She still always tried to slip half of her tips to Alice at the end of their shifts.

They both looked over their shoulders, keeping an eye out for Boris. He didn't like them talking to each other. He had figured out that they were friends and keeping them apart was another way for him to control them. It made the days pass by extremely slowly, and she always felt lonely without her. But at least Taby went home to her boyfriend. She went home alone.

Alice loved Troy, Taby's boyfriend, and she was happy that Taby had him. But she was often jealous that she didn't have someone. She had never had that.

With the way that her life had started, she hadn't had the opportunity to ever have a boyfriend. Then when she came to the city and started school, they were only after one thing. The one time that she had gone out with someone, it had ended in her losing her virginity and him never returning her calls. It had been awful.

She knew that true love and a deep connection between people existed, because it was what her parents had had. She just hadn't found it yet, and if she was honest, she wasn't sure that she was in a place to want or need that. She had goals, and she wanted to make her parents proud. She needed to concentrate on that.

***

The door chimed later in the evening. She looked up like usual but this time she paused, watching as a group of men walked in. This wasn't the first time she had seen this particular group of men, but they set her nerves on edge every time. All tall, muscular, impeccably groomed and dressed to the nines, she somehow knew they weren't the type of men she wanted to mess with.

They came in a couple of times a month and used the back room. She had never waited on them, Boris always gave the tables to Sara and moved her to another room. Something she was always thankful for. Waiting on them would have wreaked havoc on her nerves. She probably would have dropped something. Another thing to be taken out of her paycheck.

That's how she first encountered the mystery man—that was what she was calling him in her head. With pitch-black hair, he was slightly shorter than the other men in his group, but no less intimidating. He had an air about him that made him stand out from them instead, one she was sure scared most people away.

He should scare her. His commanding presence reminded her somewhat of her uncle who had been terrifying. And her past relationship hadn't exactly left her wanting another one. Yet she was drawn to the mystery man.

For months now she had watched them come in and use the back room. She had never been able to wait on them even before the new management. Every time they left, she would find herself watching them hoping for a glimpse. The mystery man would always look straight at her and nod. One simple nod. Always deliberate. Her heart would skip as his dark gaze held her captive, so hard and enthralling.

8

It wouldn't be till months later that things would finally start to come together. It had been on a rare time when Sara wasn't working with her. Sara had been on a break and she had been standing at the entrance to the restaurant, taking names for tables. It had been later in the evening and the dinner rush was well over, leaving an empty dining room.

The minute they had entered she had frozen. The man in front, larger than all the others, had given her a terrifying look. Chilling her to the bone and leaving her almost shaking. He definitely wasn't like her mystery man, whose look sent a different kind of shiver down her spine. She hadn't said anything as he asked for their table, just kept her head down and led them toward the back room.

All the while she had wondered how she was going to be able to serve them when she couldn't even seem to find her tongue. The men started seating themselves. Out of the corner of her eye she had noticed that her mystery man had paused and was staring at her. Walking up, she had handed him his menu, thinking that she needed to get her tongue unstuck.

His dark eyes had raked over her, leaving her weak in the knees, and she wasn't all that certain that she liked it. She hadn't been able to pull herself together, feeling desire and need this strong was all so new.

"Name." His voice had been deep with a timbre to it that she felt caress her skin.

"Umm ..." She was still stuck in her thoughts, not sure how to answer—not even sure what the question had been. A small smile, just a quirk of his lips, on his face as he looked at her, and she had felt her heart give another skip.

"What's your name, sweetheart?" This time his voice had been softer but slithered over her with no less effect than before.

He was a potent package, with his body, and voice. But she had found herself answering anyway.

"Alice," she had whispered. She couldn't understand how this one man could make her feel this way. Was this what her parents had felt like when they found each other? Or was this something else?

He had nodded like that was all he needed then took his seat, but his eyes continued to follow her as she handed out the menus. It had left a feeling in the pit of her stomach that she hadn't ever felt. Realistically she knew that she needed to stay away. All the men sitting around the table held an air around them that made her shiver in remembrance of her uncle and her past. It had been a sobering thought.

"I'll get my table. No need for you to steal it." Sara's scathing voice had interrupted her thoughts and she turned to see a nasty glare being sent her way.

She had tried to keep her head up high as she turned toward the door, not letting herself glance in the direction of her mystery man. It wouldn't do her any good to wish for something that she couldn't have.

She held that thought in the forefront of her mind until later that week when they were back again. She had been cleaning up the hostess station, the restaurant closed except for the group of them. She had tried to keep busy and not watch them, but as they reached the front on their way out of the restaurant Boris had pushed her ahead of them.

"Open the door for them!" he had hissed furiously in her ear as he shoved her so hard in the back that she had stumbled into the door, hitting her head. His words ringing in her ear and her head throbbing, she had pushed open the door and held it.

She could hear Boris thanking the men loudly and welcoming them back at any time, but she had kept her now pounding head down in embarrassment. Boris had always been rude and condescending, an awful boss, but he had never been physical with her before. She had tried to get her shaking under control as she watched from under her lashes as one of the men stepped through the door and seemed to look around, stepping to the side as the rest of the men filed out behind him.

Her mystery man had walked slowly out the door and stopped right in front of her. She had known that it was him, she could feel it. But she had kept her head down, not wanting to look at him. She had been so embarrassed and ashamed that she was in this position; he had to have seen what Boris had done.

She had wanted more than anything to just walk out the door and never come back, but had known that she wouldn't make it long with the money that she had. A memory from her past had flashed through her mind and she had hated that Boris had the power to bring back memories that she didn't ever want to remember.

"Look at me." His voice had cut through her memories like a knife, making her jump.

She had glanced up into eyes that blazed straight through her. A startling brown so dark at times they could appear black. They were so beautiful, and she had known that she had never seen anything like it. His gaze had lifted to her forehead where a bruise would form soon, then traveled over her head. Then with one more blazing look that shot straight through her he turned and had left, leaving her feeling bereft.

She hadn't been right ever since. Even though she had tried to forget him and the feelings she had, she couldn't. She knew it was ridiculous to be thinking of a man whose name she didn't even know.

That was then, and today was no different. She tried to catch a glimpse of him hidden behind the usual men surrounding him, but it was no use, and she mentally shook her head. This was not a time to let her mind wander; she needed to keep her wits about her if she was going to keep this job. Although she was starting to wonder if it was worth it.

Scratch that.

She knew it wasn't worth it. But school was important—she had to make her parents proud. This job was unfortunately part of it. She was so close to graduation; she just needed a little more time. She could do this. Or at least she hoped she could.

Knowing that Sara was out on her break, she scooped up their customary top-shelf bottle of bourbon and some menus and made her way back to the room. Pouring their drinks, she could feel his eyes on her, but she didn't dare look up.

She knew the kind of feeling she would get by looking into his eyes, and she couldn't focus when she was looking at him.

The last thing she needed was to drop a glass and have it taken out of her paycheck, again.

The night went fairly smoothly. Sara came back—luckily when she wasn't in the back room—and her comments were not heard by them.

Only the kitchen staff heard, snickering as she was walking away. Taby gave her a concerned glance, but they didn't stop to talk.

She just continued with her tasks.

Chapter 3

It was late.

The restaurant normally closed at eleven. But tonight, the room in the back was still being used, as more men had shown up till the whole room was full. Alice could only imagine what Sara's tips were going to be like tonight. She sighed ruefully and went back to scrubbing the floors by hand again. It had been a couple of weeks since she had seen the mystery man. She had tried not to think of him, but she hadn't been that successful, which was unfortunate, especially since she was getting ready for finals and her last weeks of the term. The whole thing was distracting her, but she couldn't help thinking about him.

She had already finished mopping the bathroom and was working in the hall, when she footsteps sounded behind her. She quickly scooted to the side and stood up. She figured it was Sara and didn't want to be kicked or stepped on—she still had the bruises from the last time. She kept her head down and her back against the wall, not wanting to incur her wrath, hoping that she could go by unseen this time but knowing that it was probably unlikely. Lately Boris had been leaving her alone, seeming to be more distracted than normal, but Sara had been doubling up her efforts.

"Why are you doing the floors by hand?" She jolted. It was the mystery man. His tone was soft but had a hard edge and she struggled to come up with an answer, afraid of disappointing him, although she had no idea why.

"Umm …" Was all that she managed. She knew why she was doing the floors by hand but telling him would be embarrassing. It would be embarrassing to tell anyone that Boris hadn't let her use a mop let alone her mystery man.

"Look at me." His voice this time was sharp, sending her eyes straight to his.

"Answer my question." She could tell that he expected an answer and would take nothing else.

"We"—she cleared her throat, her brain working overtime to come up with a response—"Lost the mop." A look of anger crossed his features but was gone quickly, replaced with a very blank look.

"Right." She could tell from his tone that he didn't believe her. He paused, still keeping his eyes arrested on hers. Her heart was beating a thousand times a minute. She wondered if he could hear it.

"Why are you not out there at the tables? I was told you were a waitress. Is that not true?" His voice was back to the deceptively soft tenor and she got the impression that he was mad, but purposely keeping his voice light. Had he checked into her? He would have had to, to know that she was a waitress. She tried to not read too much into the situation. His voice and manor, even though she felt drawn to him, still left her feeling unsettled. He was giving off the impression that he was mad, and her stomach gave a nervous flutter at the thought that he might be mad at her.

"Yes—I mean no—I mean yes, I'm a waitress." He had a small smile on his lips as she stuttered through her answer, and she felt as if she might faint.

Embarrassment and a strong pull of desire clashed inside her. He was still looking into her eyes, and she felt as if there was a string pulling her closer. He was so handsome that she was surprised that any words were coming out of her mouth at all.

"So then why?" he asked.

"I … am needed elsewhere?" She realized that her answer had come out as a question, and she mentally slapped herself. This man was handsome and made her heart beat faster, but she didn't know if she could trust him with her feelings. Whatever she said to him could come back to Boris.

At just that moment her name was yelled down the hallway, and she knew instantly this situation was about to get worse. Boris was standing in the entry to the hallway, hands on his hips, glaring at them. Or glaring at her.

"Get out of his way, girl. He doesn't have the time to deal with you. Are these floors done yet?"

It was enough to make her realize she was indeed not getting any work done, and she paled slightly.

"Sorry, sir." She kept her head down again, not wanting to make a scene in front of the mystery man.

"KITCHEN NOW!" She quickly made her escape before Boris got even angrier. She could just make out Boris apologizing to the man for her mistake as she looked over her shoulder to see them.

The man glanced at her then back at Boris, a hard look on his face. Then he turned and headed in the direction that he had started. She didn't know why she felt this crushing disappointment in her chest, since she knew he wouldn't stand up for her. Afterall, she hardly knew him. This was just a silly crush that she had, and she needed to remember that.

Giving herself another mental slap, she turned back around and walked right into Taby, who grasped her arms and steadied her. Grabbing her hand, Taby half dragged her into the kitchen that was well on its way to being shut down. Only a couple of people were left, stocking and cleaning up the last little things before being done for the night.

"Troy's on his way to pick me up but keep your head down, okay? Boris is mad. We can give you a ride since the bus isn't out this late …" She trailed off as Boris came up behind her.

"Taby, you are done for tonight. Out." He didn't say it in a way that brooked any argument, but Taby stayed put, a look of determination on her face. Scared determination, but still.

"Are you questioning me?" Boris nearly screamed in Taby's face, and she shook a little as if frightened out of her mind.

Alice knew that she wasn't the only one who had problems with Boris and Sara, and Taby needed this job just like she did. Troy had gotten out of prison for assault a couple of years ago, and although he was a completely different person, no one would hire him. He was working temp jobs, and Taby was filling the gaps with her job here while trying to finish school. She suspected that Taby didn't tell Troy all that was going on with Boris. Troy was very protective of her.

Alice glanced over at Taby and, although she was grateful that Taby was trying to help her, she couldn't put her in this position. Boris was angrier than usual, and she knew that whatever was going to happen wasn't going to be good.

"It's okay," she whispered to her. Giving her a reassuring smile, Alice hugged her and gently pushed her toward the door.

"Troy should be here to pick you up. I'll call a taxi; you go ahead and go."

Taby looked doubtful but ran to the back and grabbed her stuff, making a sign that she would call her. Then she left out the back door with one more quick worried glance her way.

She was standing between a table and the grill. The only way out was behind her. She was starting to fear her situation now that Taby was gone. She couldn't see anyone else in the restaurant and knew that she was in trouble, but before she could make a break for it, Boris reached out and grabbed her wrist.

Hard.

"You stupid little shit! You just have to get in the way, don't you! Well, you have two options, give me what I want or"— a greasy smile came over his sweaty face—"give me what I want."

She knew that turning him down was a bad idea, it had only enraged him last time, but she wasn't about to give in. She would rather be fired and take her chances. "No," she said, shaking with a mixture of fear and anger. Boris's smile turned nasty and he tightened his grip on her wrist, before he forced her hand down flat on the still hot grill.

Hot, searing pain shot through her hand and she screamed. Bobby came running from the back, but Boris had already let go, taking a step away from her, a nasty smirk still on his face. She yanked her hand away and held it to her chest. Crying and trying not to scream, she bit her lip. She watched him warily, fearing that he would do something else.

"Better watch what you are doing there, Alice. Wouldn't want you to get hurt." With that, he walked away as Old Bobby rushed up to her.

"You okay, girl? What'd he do?" His slight Irish accent made him sound angrier, but his face showed nothing but concern. He started to reach for her, but she shook her head and stepped back. He straightened, studying her.

"That stupid ..." He took a hard breath and seemed to be on the verge of an outburst. Then he calmed and started again.

"He seems to have it out for you, girl. You need to get out of here and get a different job. Ain't nothing here good for you." She had a sudden flash of the mysterious man, before shaking it away. This was a problem that she had to deal with herself. Nobody, not even Taby could help her with this.

"I can't find anything that will work with my school schedule. But I'm trying."

She knew that her excuses sounded just as lame as they really were. There was a line that had been crossed tonight. She was going to have to work up the courage to quit. Her parents would understand, she hoped.

They stood there quietly for a moment, even though they were the only two people left in the restaurant. Her nerves settled, knowing that she was finally safe now that Boris was gone. Old Bobby was more of a grandpa to her and Taby than anything else.

They didn't know much about him, but he was always there to help and lend a hand. As soon as she had that thought, he patted her shoulder and told her that he would finish up. She didn't even think twice about trying to talk him out of it. Her hand was throbbing.

She just hoped that she didn't have to go to the emergency room. She didn't have insurance or the money for it. She grabbed her stuff and headed out. It was going to be a long walk home.

18

Chapter 4

The next day she almost didn't get to school on time. The late night and the two-hour walk home, when she hadn't been able to get an Uber, had done her in.

She was so close to being done though, so she got up and showered and rewrapped her throbbing hand. It looked twice as bad in the morning light; it was red and swollen, with small blisters covering her whole palm.

She knew that this was the end, that she couldn't stay there any longer, no matter how badly she needed the money. She had four more days till payday and she only worked one of them. She was scared that she wasn't going to find another position, but at this point she knew she had to take that chance. If she stayed, there was no telling what would happen.

She walked onto to campus where a waiting Taby searched frantically for her. Taby relaxed when she saw her.

"God, I was so worried." Taby reached out and wrapped her in a hug.

"I'm okay." Her reassurances were lost when Taby caught sight of her hand. Alice quickly dropped it from Taby's arm, but it was too late.

"What happened?" she asked, her voice breaking. When Alice didn't answer she took a step back, shaking her head.

"It's okay, Taby, don't—"

"I left you there," she bemoaned.

Alice shook her head. "No. I told you to go. Listen, it's okay. I'm quitting, okay? I'll be out of there tomorrow on payday. And I think you should come, too."

At that, Taby's face lit up.

"I didn't get a chance to call you last night," Taby said as they began walking to their first class. "Troy may have a new job. He's been working security for this company on trial for a little bit now. And he said that the trial may be up, and they want him to stay on!"

"Taby, that's great!" She was happy for them. This meant so much to them. "What's the pay? Will you be able to go to school full time?"

"Yes! It pays so well that I won't have to work! And Troy says it comes with a place to stay so we can move out of that group rental now!" Alice jumped forward and hugged Taby.

For the last few months, Taby and Troy had been renting a room in a group rental across town. It was them and three other men, and both Troy and Taby were uncomfortable living there.

"Oh Taby, I'm so happy for you! See? You don't need to worry! Everything will be okay now!"

They linked their arms and walked into their class, heading toward the back where they always sat. She still couldn't believe that school was almost done. She only had one more semester. She sighed, looking around and wondering if she would miss it. She would miss seeing Taby. They had been pretty much inseparable since their freshman year. And although Alice was almost done, Taby was taking fewer classes at a time and still had some time to go.

Picking up her notes after class, she thought about what she needed to do for the day before work. She only had one class today.

"Here, this is for you. I am not taking no for an answer. It's not much but that's all I made in tips last night, okay? Soon we will be good, and I know you don't have food right now, okay? Love you!" Taby said handing her an envelope. Before Alice could say anything, Taby was rushing out the door.

She opened the envelope and counted the dollar bills. Sixty dollars! Taby was right, it wasn't much but to Alice right now it was like she had won the lottery. Maybe she could make rent now, maybe even get a hamburger for dinner!

Thinking about the rent reminded her that she needed to pay her next month's term. It was her last one and she was excited to pay it off and be done with it. She wasn't sure where she was going to work, but that was why she went with a degree in business. Other than being good with numbers, it was a good degree for several positions. Soon she would be able to apply to jobs that were in her field, and when school was done she could work full time.

She walked out of the financial aid office, a pang of sadness in her chest. That was the last of her parents' trust, but she had done it. Her last semester was paid for. Ever since she had turned eighteen and it was given to her, she had budgeted closely. Getting secondhand books and even working two jobs last year so that she could make it work, so she could finish. It had always been her parents dream for her to go to college, and they must have worked hard to save. They never did have much, and in reality they didn't leave her much, but it had been enough.

She had just enough to make rent and pay for another semester's bus pass. Food would come later. She smiled, tipping her head up toward the sky and breathing in the crisp fall air. Finally, things were looking up for her.

***

Two days later, and she was still on a high from paying her tuition. It was hard to be sad when her dreams were coming true. Sara seemed to be in a particularly awful mood and Boris was on a rampage, but it didn't matter to her. Taby had shown up to work, stating that they were moving the next day. She was so happy about Taby and her school that she was practically dancing around the restaurant.

Thoughts of finally finishing school and moving somewhere else were playing in her head as she scrubbed floors and finished her menial tasks all evening. Where would she go? After her parents died she had gone to live with her uncle. But after everything that had happened, she would never go back there.

She had been lucky to find out about her trust fund. So she grabbed the papers and left. She ended up here, picking the city at random. Before it wouldn't have mattered where she was living, but now she didn't know if she could leave Taby and Troy. Maybe if she was in a better part of town she wouldn't mind it so much. Yes, she thought that was what she should do. There were lots of businesses downtown. She knew that she could find a job there eventually, and living somewhere closer to the better part of town, even if it took her closer to Chicago, was better than where she was.

She grimaced as her hand twinged. She had been scrubbing floors for a while now and knew that she needed to change the bandage. Luckily, she had stopped and picked up some pain medicine on the way to work so it didn't hurt too bad.

However, by nine that night her hand was throbbing, and the bandage looked horrible, but she didn't have anything to change it with. Boris hadn't wanted to give her the med-kit, saying that she wasn't out with customers so it didn't matter.

She was wondering if she could sneak into Boris' office and make off with the first aid kit. She figured it probably wasn't worth it, it probably wouldn't even have anything she could use. He was too cheap to actually have put stuff in it. Taby came running around the corner, startling her from her thoughts with a weird look on her face.

"Alice!" she whisper-yelled. "They asked for you and Boris is on a tear! So is Sara!" Then as fast as she came she was gone, being her usually dramatic self. Alice smirked, wondering what she was going on about but continued to stack the dirty plates for Old Bobby.

"Alice!" Boris yelled out, and she instantly wished that Taby had stayed to explain better.

"Yes, sir?" she asked. She didn't have to deal with this much longer. When her shift was over and he handed out the paychecks, she could quit. She couldn't let him get to her. She had learned long ago that men like him were dangerous when they knew that they had power over you. That you feared them.

"Get out there. They are asking for you. And I swear if you say one thing …" He left off what would happen, but she could well imagine. She started shaking as fear set in, not knowing what was going on. She didn't know who was asking for her, but the way Boris was acting she couldn't mess this up.

It all became clear as Boris dragged her to the front of the restaurant. It was almost nine-thirty, and the restaurant closed

23

at ten that night, so there weren't that many people there let alone anyone coming in to eat. It didn't matter, though, because there was the mystery man with his entourage. The mystery man was at the front and several men, more than normal, were filing in behind him. As soon as she came falling into the room, his dark eyes found hers and never left

She had a sinking feeling about what had happened. They asked for her to be their waitress! Sara's mean look directed at her clued her in to the fact she was right. Sara took one more glance at the men then marched toward the back, knocking into her on the way.

"Good luck—they won't be tipping your fat ass!" she said as she left in a huff.

"Get out there and remember: Don't say anything," Boris whispered in her ear. His meaty hand was wrapped around her arm in a painful grip. She tried not to wince as he gave a little tug to reinforce what he said. She looked up and her gaze immediately swept toward the mystery man to see that he was watching Boris with a cold look. His gaze swung to her and he frowned as she dropped her eyes in embarrassment. Sometimes she really wished that she was tougher and could stand up to people. She shrugged out of Boris' grip and picked up a stack of menus.

"This way, gentlemen," she murmured, and walked them toward the back room.

Chapter 5

Dominic Mancini watched as his little Alice walked toward the back room where they always sat. He couldn't keep his eyes off her form as a shot of fire went straight to his dick. She had nicely rounded hips and a tapered waist, perfect for him to grasp from behind. With her small and feminine features, she reminded him of a delicate little bird. Beautiful, flighty, and a gift to those around them.

It had taken him a few months of watching her around the restaurant, but soon he realized that he wasn't going to be able to shake her till he had her under him. Till he got his hands on and dick in that curvy body of hers. But he hadn't pursued anything like he normally would; somehow, he knew that she wasn't a one and done type of girl. Then he heard her say her name for the first time and it was like everything shifted.

His world twisted, crashing against the barriers that were his heart. Instantly he was taken, swept up in an obsession that he knew deep in his soul he would never lose. He let it fill him up and consume him. Relished it. He knew then and there that she was going to be his, he just had to be patient.

In the meantime, he had to do with the reports from his men and the dishwasher, Bobby. He had hired the man to look after her when he couldn't be there. He knew that Boris was a mean fuck, and he hadn't liked leaving her there when he couldn't protect her. But with his business in the situation that it was, his hands had been tied.

"Are you ready for this man," Danny whispered from beside him as they sat down at their table. Alice had given them their menus and after a word from Rick, had left them alone. The rest of their party would be in soon enough. For now, they would just have to wait.

"Ready for it to be over?" he asked, turning his attention back to Danny now that Alice was no longer in the room.

"Ready to have a life. To be free from all of this. This is a big night, for all of us," Danny said as he looked to the men around him before answering.

"Yes I am, but more so that I'm finally giving my grandfather his wish. This is something that he had wanted as long as I can remember." He sighed as he thought over the momentous of this occasion. In more ways than one. Yes, this was for his family, but it was also for him.

For her.

After tonight there would be nothing standing in his way from going after her.

He wasn't about to tell his men that.

"We all miss him," Rick said from the other side of him, misinterpreting his silence for grief over his grandfather.

Rick and Danny were two of his closest friends. Had been with him since he was a teenager. They had grown up together, and he knew that they missed his grandfather just as much as he did. They were all so different, but they seemed to work together. Danny was the people person. He could talk your ear off, charm the socks off anyone, and had a revolving door of women that came to him.

If Danny was the people person and womanizer, Rick was the quiet one. He never spoke unless it was something important, but he caught more than he let on. He was always watching.

Then there was himself. He had turned out to be the semi leader of the group. As much because of his position in the Familia as his controlling nature. But it had worked for all three of them and they had fast developed a deep friendship. A friendship that had lasted through all the trouble of leading a life with the Familia.

Tonight, though, was the end of it all.

His father had spent his whole life cultivating relationships and stashing favors for the very reason that he was in this room tonight. He was meeting with the soon-to-be head boss, Ivanov, to sign over the last of his holdings here in the city. Then it would only be about packing and deciding where they wanted to go from here. He had known that this moment was coming for a while, but other than setting up his business and nightclubs he hadn't really planned for a future.

His father had also made sure that he had been able to support himself outside of the Familia for this very reason. So he had built up a line of very successful nightclubs. All different, all in different parts of the country, all catering to different clientele.

They were successful.

But more importantly, they would support him well beyond his means after his ties to the Familia were cut. He wasn't even upset to be losing the one located here in the city through the trade-off. It was well worth the effort to be free of the strings of the Familia lifestyle.

For as long as he could remember, his grandfather had talked about how the Familia wasn't a place to have a real life, a family. He had talked about what an honor it was to be part of the Familia, but that he wanted different for his family. After all, Dominic's grandmother couldn't stand the lifestyle and had left shortly after his father had been born. It had been further enforced when Dominic's mother had died in a shoot-out over territory. His heart hurt at the thought of never getting to know her. He had been three when she died, and it made what his grandfather had wanted even more important.

It had always amazed him how his grandfather could be so proud of something and still not want it for his own family. He had passed before he had been able to see this dream come true—his grandson turning over the mantle. His father had already retired and gone on an extended vacation with his new wife, leaving the final details to Dominic. There had been many conflicts with turning over everything, but with his father's connections and favors owed that had been called in it was now time. It was a perfect ending to what his grandfather had started.

What he hadn't counted on was meeting the sweet little angel of a waitress in the restaurant. They had been meeting Ivanov here for months now, fine-tuning everything from his clubs, to turning over his underworld contacts. Ivanov said that the manager was on the payroll and was trustworthy. Wanting the meetings to go smoothly, Dominic had agreed. Even if he didn't agree with how the staff was treated here, especially his Alice. She was terrified. He could see it, sense it. With the way that Boris treated the girl, how she cowered before him, the fat fuck was about to get it if he didn't watch what he was doing. He might not be taking over the Familia anymore, but that didn't mean that he was someone to fuck with.

There was something in her gaze that made him want to wrap her up in cotton and carry her off. But he needed to tread carefully, at least until everything was signed tonight. His father and the Familia had worked hard to get him here, and he couldn't blow it for anything.

Even her.

At least not yet.

After the incident where he had found her mopping the floor on her hands and knees, he had been angry enough to murder someone. But he had clenched his fists and walked away. That was when he started paying Bobby to look out for her.

When he had gotten home, he had one of his men do a check on her. Her parents had died when she was sixteen and she had gone to live with an uncle. There was a black spot for a few years and then she showed up halfway across the country, enrolled in a school. Normally that wouldn't arouse too much suspicion, but with his job he worked with the unsavory and didn't take anything at face value. She wasn't in any database anywhere in that time. No doctors, no schools, nothing. And the uncle's name came back blank.

It had set his nerves on edge. Her uncle's name, George Beckman, was a fake identity. That, coupled with the look that she had in her eyes, spoke of a leeriness and fear that he knew too well. He had caused that look on men before. Something had happened in her life, he just needed to figure it out. And he would.

She was shy and unsure; he could see it in the way that she watched people. The only time he had seen her light up was when she was around the other girl. Taby, he thought her name was. He wanted her to look at him like that. Like her world was perfect and right, with him there next to her. He knew that he would get it. He always got what he wanted.

Besides, the transfer was almost over. Only a few more hours and he would finally be free of his ties to the Familia and he could get his girl. She just didn't know it yet. He smiled.

The fun was just beginning.

Chapter 6

Alice walked the group of men toward the back and showed them to a table. She watched as all of them sat, each one dressed in a crisp and clean suit. The air around them was electric and biting, different than other nights. She also noticed that they sat on two sides of the table, not together. It almost seemed as if they were making a statement as to the fact that they were not together, even if they were sitting at the same table.

She shook her head, admonishing herself. It didn't matter. This was a large group and she needed the tips, so she got busy passing out the menus, trying to hide her hand the best she could. The bandage was really dirty, but until she got home she wouldn't be able to change it.

She had been able to pay her rent with the money that Taby had passed her. But she would need food, and if she could get a tip from this table maybe she could get some dinner tonight. She had run out of ramen yesterday morning. So she didn't need them seeing it and being disgusted. She *really* needed the tips.

She gave them a moment and went to the side table to pour them their drinks. She knew from their previous visits and having to stock the room that they all liked a certain brand of top-shelf bourbon, except for one man who liked vodka. Before she could figure out how she was going to carry a tray of drinks and serve them with only one hand Taby slipped into the room. Grabbing one of the trays they worked together to serve everyone.

"I'm leaving," Taby whispered, looking at her with concern.

"Of course. Don't worry. I'll be fine."

"No, sweetie. I'm *leaving*," Taby whispered again, and Alice felt a sadness come over. She wasn't going to miss the job, but she was definitely going to miss seeing her friend all the time.

"Troy doesn't want me here anymore. And really I don't want to be here either," she continued gently, still looking worried. Taby was clearly thinking about Boris and what would happen to her if she stayed the rest of the night. But if she left now Boris wouldn't give her her paycheck.

"I paid my last semester today," she said, trying to cheer her friend up. She got what she wanted when Taby smiled and nodded. When Taby looked over her shoulder at the group, Alice was reminded that she needed to get back to work.

"I've got to get to work, okay?" She reached out with her good hand and hugged her friend.

"You know you can stay with Troy and me now that we have a place, right?" Alice looked up at Taby to see that she still wasn't giving it up.

"Taby honey, you and Troy are going to be busy in that place." She wiggled her eyebrows to make her point, and Taby chuckled just like she had wanted. "But I know that you're there for me, okay?" Taby nodded and they stepped back from each other.

"Taby!" Boris was right behind them. They had been so engrossed in their talk that they hadn't noticed him coming up behind them.

"Why the fuck are you still here? And you!" He rounded on her. "Serve those goddamn drinks." Boris turned on his heel and marched out of the room.

Giving one last smile to Taby, knowing that she would see her soon, she grabbed the tray and hustled over to the table. She started handing out drinks, trying not to look up. She could feel the mysterious man's eyes on her as she moved around the table, but she didn't dare look up. How he made her feel was dangerous. She hadn't even told Taby about it, too scared to voice her feelings.

"Leave us. We will call when you are needed," said one of the men in the room, his voice cold, and she quickly made her exit.

**

The evening progressed slowly. She tried to not stay in the room unless absolutely necessary. Not only were there more men than normal but the mood was different. After several drinks and a round of appetizers ordered for the whole table, several of the men left. She was slightly alarmed at how her thoughts automatically went to him, and if he was leaving, too.

Not working at the restaurant anymore meant that she would probably never see him again, and it scared her how sad that made her. But when she went to check in on them, she found that he was still there with a few of the men who were always with him. Walking into the room to check their drinks, they all seemed to be in a good mood, patting each other on the back and cheering her mystery man on.

"Hey there! Champagne, woman! We need to toast!" a man called, and she slightly remembered someone calling him Danny. She smiled at his over-the-top manner and nodded, going to the back to get one of the chilled bottles.

She filled their glasses and started to clear the table as she watched out of the corner of her eye. Another man who looked a lot like Danny but had a slightly taller build stood up and clinked his glass to get everyone's attention!

"Here's to Dominic! Following his grandfather's wish and getting us the fuck out of the Familia!" He cheered and everyone joined in.

Her mysterious man was sitting at the head of the table, silently watching the rest of the group. He smiled at the toast and raised his glass. She stood transfixed behind the bar as the smile came over his face. She had never seen him smile before, and right now his face was alight with joy at whatever had transpired tonight. His face was always so handsome that it made her heart stutter, but when he smiled it transformed it into something that she didn't even have words for. She couldn't help but stare.

She kept refilling drinks long into the night. The kitchen had closed down but Boris didn't kick them out, content to let them drink. He went back into his office and she stayed in the back room, standing in the corner, waiting to refill their drinks.

As the men shouted for another refill, she loaded her tray to make another round. Things were getting rowdy now, Danny and another man cracking jokes and making everyone laugh. What drew her attention was that, while everyone else was celebrating, one man sat toward the back of the table and seemed to be brooding. But nobody seemed to be paying him any mind.

Her mystery man just continued to sit back and watch everyone. He continued to smile at all the laughing and joking around him. But he seemed content to sit back and let it happen around him. There were only six men left now, but they were making enough noise for it to sound like a hundred. She found herself trying not to laugh at their antics, as the night continued on.

She made her way around the table, dropping off another round of drinks. She took the last drink off the tray and set it in front of her mystery man, at the same time surveying the food to see if they needed anything else. That was why, when she started to move away, she was stopped by his commanding voice.

"Stop." It wasn't said menacingly or angrily, but it was definitely a command, and she froze.

"Show me your hands," he said in the same commanding tone. She looked into his eyes, and although she had been serving drinks all night, he didn't have an iota of unsteadiness to him. He looked to be completely sober.

She reached out slowly and showed him her bandage-free hand, her shaking hand betraying her nerves. A flash of anger shot through his eyes and she took a small step back.

She suddenly realized that her little crush had lulled her into a sense of security. That she didn't *really* know him. Didn't know what he would do when angry.

"The other hand." His voice held none of the anger that was on his face. She still hesitated though.

She felt a shot of panic go through her at what he wanted. She had been successful all night in hiding her hand. She was so close to being done working here and getting out, and if she made a scene, she might never get her last paycheck.

"Umm ..." she stuttered, trying to figure out if this man or Boris was the worse option.

35

"Now!"

She jumped at his harsh tone, dropping the tray. She tried to reach out for it but he grabbed her injured hand in a firm grip stopping her, and she froze watching as the tray fell to the floor with a clatter.

"What happened?" he asked softly, still staring down at her bandaged hand that was dirtier than a mop cloth.

She heard his words, but she was frozen, staring at the tray on the ground, a deer caught in the headlights. Her mind was working overtime, but she didn't think she could utter a sound if her life depended on it.

"It's okay," he murmured at her pause, but all she could do was just shake her head

Fear was clawing its way out of the little box that she kept it in, choking her, and she started to shake. Memories were fighting their way out, coming up to consume her. Panic started to fill her as, instead of the mystery man standing in front of her, she saw her uncle. Her breath sawed in and out of her burning lungs.

"Sir." They all looked up when they heard Old Bobby at the entrance to the room. She hadn't even realized that he was still there, as late as it was.

"Is this why you called me?" her mystery man asked, and Bobby nodded. He didn't look frightened, though, but she couldn't figure out why.

Called him? Why would Bobby have called him? How did they even know each other? Wondering about Bobby helped her fear fade a little enough to start thinking rationally again. She hoped that Bobby would help her if she really needed it.

"He forced her hand onto the grill, sir." Grumbles came from the men around them and two stood up so fast that their chairs flung out behind them, clattering to the floor.

Slowly the mystery man holding her hand stood.

"What?" The mood in the room dipped, as if the temperature had suddenly dropped ten degrees. She shivered. Bobby nodded, and in a sudden burst of fury the man dropped her hand and grabbed his drink, flinging it against the wall.

"Bring me that fucker!"

Three men shot out of the room, their feet pounding down the hall. Old Bobby looked at her one more time before he turned and walked away. But none of that mattered. Alice was so shocked and scared, that she took an involuntary step back, and his eyes swung toward her. They were filled with such hate and anger that she gasped.

The man stood watching her, his gaze burning into her when he muttered low as if he knew exactly what she was doing to do. As if his words could stop the panic and fear clawing her insides.

"Do not." His voice was rumbled, his eyes boring into her. But all she could see was the glass smashing against the wall. It kept replaying in her mind over and over. It was mixing with her memories, her past, and she kept seeing her blood, splattered and running down the wall instead of the alcohol.

He tried to grab her before but she managed to avoid him as she fled the room.

"Alice!" His was voice was booming and only urged her on more. "Follow her!"

She reached the side door that would put her out on the street. She only hoped that it would give her the head start that she needed. She might not be much, but she was fast. She had run track before her parents passed.

As she came around the corner she saw that luck was on her side as the bus pull up toward its stop down the road. Pumping her legs hard she made it just before the operator closed the door. Jumping on and flinging herself into a seat in the back, she pulled her knees to her chest and broke down crying.

Chapter 7

It was a while before she calmed down enough to stop crying. She sat up and tried to brush her tears away while looking out the window and saw that she was close to her stop. Getting off the bus, she shivered at the cold. October was still early, but it certainly wasn't a time to go without her coat.

Her coat!

Alice stopped as she realized that she hadn't taken anything with her from the restaurant. She had left her coat and purse there. Her keys were there! Her phone! How was she supposed to get into her apartment? She sighed, knowing that the rest of her evening just got a lot more complicated.

The landlord decided that for her last twenty dollars he would let her in. She resisted the urge to not roll her eyes at him. He wasn't a creeper just a lazy old man, but right now she was just thankful that he was helping her. But it was a costly mistake; that last twenty dollars was going to be her food money. She inwardly winced, thinking of the few packages of soda crackers in her cupboard. She might have a little powdered milk and cereal left, but she would have to worry about that and everything else later.

What she needed was a shower and a new bandage on her now throbbing hand. Then she would figure out how to get in touch with Bobby. Maybe he had picked up her stuff after her crazy dash out of the restaurant. She was still shaken up, thinking about what had happened in the restaurant. There was no way that Boris was going to let her work her last day now. She could only hope that he would give her a chance to get her last paycheck. Although she really didn't know how to go about getting it. It was too late to worry about it now—she would just have to figure it out later.

She was also confused. Why had that man acted like that? Who was he, and what did he want with her? She knew that he must be powerful; she could not only feel it but see it with the way he acted and how his men treated him.

She could never trust a man that lashed out like that. Not that it mattered. There was no way that he was interested in her, so what did he want then? Just a night in her bed? No, she couldn't trust him. She had once trusted a man who was supposed to take care of her, and the damage he caused would forever sit with her. She shuddered at the thought. Walking to the bathroom, she started the shower. Thinking about the days after she had left that life behind.

Her uncle had been a very mysterious man, a very secretive man. She had gone to live with him after her parents died. She never could figure out what he did. He had several names that he had gone by and had always been suspicious. But as a child she had never questioned it too much.

One time after she had used the phone to call a new friend at school, he had freaked out and locked her in her room. That soon became normal, and before long he was telling people that he was homeschooling her. But it had all been a lie.

When she had been about to turn eighteen, he had started telling her about what he was going to do to her, let his men do to her. He had loved to use his words to taunt her. His abuse had also started to become physical, and she was grateful that she had escaped before it had gone any further.

One day the mailman came with a certified letter for her and she had to sign for it. It was the paperwork for a trust set up for her by her parents. Until then she hadn't had a clue that it had existed. It was the first sign of hope that she had been given.

She was lucky that nobody had been home when it came. Who knew what her uncle would have done. She couldn't trust anyone except the old lady who came and cleaned the house. She had been a nice woman who often snuck her extra food and let her out of her room when she had the chance. She had been there when Alice had gotten the paperwork and had been the one to help her leave. Pushing her out the door with a number to get in touch with her once she was safe. She had never even known her name.

Two months after she left she called the number. The lady's son answered and told her that the woman had died of suicide. She had known better. She had helped Alice escape and paid for it with her life.

This was why she could never trust any man. Not fully. She wouldn't go back to that. Not after the price that had already been paid. She shrugged, trying to shove the memories away, and stepped into the shower, letting the hot water cleanse her of the day. She needed sleep, then a plan.

***

A slight knocking woke her. She lay in bed, thinking that it was probably the neighbors' door, but it came again. Not knowing what time it was or how long she had been asleep she rubbed at her head and eyes, wishing that whoever was there would go away. She usually had her phone for a clock, but she could still tell that it was late. After another louder, more forceful, knock sounded she slowly climbed out of bed, grabbed a sweatshirt, and pulled it over her head.

She didn't know who would be knocking on her door, let alone at this hour. Nobody but Taby knew where she lived. She made it about halfway across the room when the intermittent knocking turned to a constant pounding and she paused in the middle of the room.

That really didn't sound good. She wondered if it was smart to even open the door, especially with everything that had happened tonight.

She jumped and took a step back when the slamming started. It was as if they were trying to break her door down. She didn't think that opening that door was going to be a good idea. Would Taby had told Troy about where she was living? Could it be him maybe trying to check on her? But even as she had the thought, she knew that it wasn't him. He probably wouldn't break her door down without calling out her name.

The pounding came again, along with a voice that caused her to freeze and her breath to stall in her lungs, chilling her.

"I know you're in there. Open the door now." She gasped. It was him! The man from the restaurant! How had he found her?

"Now!" he yelled again, adding more pounding.

The neighbor across the hall opened his door and started yelling. And she knew that if she didn't do something quick someone would call the police or she would get thrown out. She quickly walked to the door, her heart in her throat. She wished she had her phone so she could call somebody.

She didn't have any chain or peephole on her door so she had no choice but to open the door, and when she did, he didn't waste any time shoving it open and barging in. She stepped back so as to not get run over and stayed behind the edge of the door. At least it was a little protection.

She watched as his eyes did a quick search of the room, sneering at the mattress on the floor before coming to her. She took a step back as she realized that he was angry again. She didn't think he was a person she wanted to piss off, so she edged back with the door in front of her even more. However, when more men filed in behind him, one grabbed the door and yanked it out of her hands, slamming it shut. Her eyes widened as she did a sweep of all of them. She didn't like where this was heading. She felt cornered, her eyes darting to each man, trying to get a read on the situation.

"Eyes on me!" the mystery man barked. She jerked her eyes back to him, afraid to defy him. This situation was quickly turning out to be a nightmare.

"This is where you live?" She could hear the disdain in his tone, and it made her ashamed and then angry that she felt ashamed at all.

It wasn't the best place, but it was a roof over her head and it was hers. And she took good care of it. It was clean and always smelled good. It didn't matter that some of the windows were cracked or the few kitchen cabinets were hanging sideways. She was trying, darn it! She twisted her hands together to keep them from shaking as she nodded, while he seemed to do more of an assessment around the room, as if looking for something.

Then suddenly, as if coming to a conclusion, he nodded once. His shoulders dropped slightly, and his face lost some of its angry expression as it became a blank mask. She wasn't sure what was worse. She didn't like that she couldn't get a read on him.

"You're coming with me," he said as he reached forward and grabbed her arm, pulling her behind him.

"Gather anything that's personal, leave the rest," he muttered to the men beside him as he walked by them, dragging her.

"Yes, sir," one man said back. He was tall and with blond hair and reminded her of a bulky version of Thor.

When he started to drag her out of the room she finally came to her senses, frantically pulling at her arm, trying to stop him.

"Listen, I'm sorry but I can't go with you. I don't know you and ..." She rushed the words out while still pulling unsuccessfully at her arm in his grasp.

He halted and turned toward her, causing her to slam into him. It didn't seem to bother him, though, as he used the momentum to back her up against the wall in the hallway, one arm coming up to lean against the building by her head. His body was flush against her, his hand holding hers, resting on his chest, the only thing between them. She felt her breath stutter as his face dipped down, coming in closer, and at his quiet words, she felt her eyes go big.

"I will explain everything later. Right now you need to know three things. One, you are coming with me. Two, I take care of everything that is mine. And three ..." He paused as his eyes skimmed over her face. "You are mine." With that, he proceeded to drag her out the lobby door. She was so stunned she didn't get a grip till they were out the door and almost to the parking lot.

"Wait …" He stopped and heaved a great sigh, as if this was testing the limited amount of patience he had. Then she realized that she probably was. But she couldn't just go with him.

"I don't know you," she whispered, wishing her voice was stronger.

She really needed to work on that, she thought.

He seemed to ponder her words for a moment then reached into his pocket and dug out a sleek black phone. He pressed a few buttons and put it to her ear. She tried to get him to let go of her hand so that she could hold it but he simply stepped into her space and held it for her, continuing to hold on to her hand while she cradled her burned hand to her chest. She realized just how close he was to her again. Did the man not believe in personal space? Even though he wasn't touching her, it was still very intimate. A hello jolted her out of her thoughts to the person on the other end of the phone.

"Troy?" she asked incredulously. What the heck was going on?

"God, Alice! Taby is freaking out! Are you okay? You're with Dominic, right?"

"Dominic?" she asked, confused. Was that mystery man's name?

"The man from … Listen, Taby wants to talk to you, okay? Listen to me. Dominic will take care of you, okay? I've known him since I was a kid. He's a good man, okay? He won't hurt you. Do you understand?"

"Umm … Yes." Her answer sounded just like she felt. Unsure and overwhelmed. She was supposed to go with him?

Troy knew him so that had to mean that she was safe, right? Her head was spinning from the new turn of events, and she wasn't sure of anything right now.

"Alice?" At the sound of Taby's voice, some of her tension leaked away and she couldn't help but lean into the man a little as relief surged through her. It had to be okay now. Taby would scream the city down if she was in any trouble.

"It's okay. I promise. I talked to Troy, okay? He knows Dominic. Trust him, Alice. He told me what happened with your hand, and Boris is mad. I need you to be safe. We don't move till tomorrow and then you can stay with us." Taby kept talking, but she was talking so fast Alice only heard a few pieces.

She was having a hard time keeping up with everything that was happening, but she got that both Troy and Taby knew him and they thought that he would take care of her for now. That had to mean something. Taby didn't know of her past, but she knew enough to know that she was shy and unsure around men. Taby would never put her in a position that would jeopardize that fine line that even Taby knew she walked every day.

"Promise?" she whispered, staring at Dominic's chest, unwilling to look him in the eye. Once again, she realized Taby was right and that she really needed to work on that confrontation thing.

"Yes, I promise. And you can call me whenever you need to, okay? Dominic has our number. Okay?"

"Okay. Thank you."

"Don't thank me. Just trust him. He will explain everything. Oh! And I went and got your bag from Bobby. He got it out for you, but we couldn't find your coat."

She sighed as another weight was lifted. She wasn't sure what she would have done without her wallet. Her coat was a big loss, one that she couldn't afford going into winter but one that she could deal with.

He suddenly lifted the phone away from her ear and started talking, asking for Troy again, but he didn't step back.

His answers were short and almost angry, but when she hesitantly looked into his eyes she saw that he was staring gently down at her. He quickly finished the call and then just stood there, looking at her. His arm was still wrapped around her, their bodies near flush to each other, and she couldn't help the thought that he was big. And tall. She wanted to melt into him as a feeling of safety came over her.

Even if she didn't know him, she felt as if everything was okay right now. It was confusing because her head was screaming at her to back away while her heart was wanting to lean in even more. She didn't know which one to follow, so she studied his eyes, hoping for an answer.

"Do you remember what I told you?" He was talking in a gentle but firm voice, as if trying to make his words all that more meaningful.

His hand came up, cupping her cheek, but his hand was so large and her face so small that his fingers reached clear to the back of her neck and his thumb brushed the edge of her lips. His gaze was so intense that she had a hard time keeping her eyes on him. She knew he was trying to get her to remember something, but what was it?

"Yes," she whispered back, giving him the answer he was looking for but still not sure of the actual answer. She didn't want to say no and upset him again, though. He was starting to calm

47

down and was a little less scary than before. She didn't want to irk the beast inside.

"And what did I say?"

One thing he had said had really struck something inside her. So that's what she went with.

"That you take care of what is yours." He gave her a small, gentle smile; his thumb still moving over her cheek, a sign of approval that she had remembered right.

"Yes, baby. And you're mine." A statement, not a question, as he searched her face for something she didn't know if she had.

"Do you feel okay, now that your girl knows where you're going?"

She nodded, still slightly alarmed that he knew so much about her but reassured with Troy telling her he knew him and where she would be. All this still didn't answer all her questions, though. She opened her mouth to ask him, but he stopped her with a finger to her lips.

"Shh." His voice was back to that forceful yet gentle sound that she was starting to like.

"I know it will take time. But someday you will be calling me for reassurances, not anybody else." The possessive tone in his words caressed her insides, as she wondered just what rabbit hole she had fallen down.

"In the meantime, I'm taking care of you. And this place is not fit for gutter trash." He said the last with a sneer and a chin jerk toward the building behind her, letting his opinion of her home be very apparent.

"Let alone someone like you." He wrapped his arm around her and guided her to the car waiting for them in the parking lot.

Chapter 8

She was sitting in the back seat next to him, watching the scenery pass by. He let her have her space. He knew that pushing his way in wasn't going to get him anywhere, even it was against his nature to go slow. It was almost killing him to not touch her, but he had freaked her out enough with his outburst in the restaurant.

It had been hard enough not being able to do anything these last few weeks. Just sitting there knowing that she was his, but unable to claim her. When he had gotten the call from Bobby that something was wrong he figured it was something that needed to be dealt with, but he never imagined that it was going to be as bad as it actually was.

So he had held off. That was his mistake. He had to give her credit, she had hidden her hand fairly well. It wasn't until she was serving drinks when they were celebrating that he saw the bandage and realized that she was hurt. When Bobby had said that the fucker Boris had held her hand down on the grill, he had seen red. He had lashed out and thrown his drink against the wall, his temper getting the best of him and scaring her in the process. He had always had a nasty temper and was known to let it rip. But doing it in front of her had been another mistake.

He was racking them up.

He had let her go, thinking that maybe some time away from him would let her settle down. Besides, he had had a man following her so she would be safe and not alone. But the look on her face as she fled was one that would stay with him. It was one that he knew personally and had seen on the faces of others.

It wasn't him that she saw when he threw that glass. It was a memory of something else. What, he didn't know, but he would find out. She had been hurt in the past, and that thought alone made him angry enough to smash the window next to him. Was it that fucker Boris, or was it something else in her past? Maybe something happened when she was with her uncle for a time. That squirrelly fucker kept eluding his man. They couldn't find anything on him, and he didn't like not knowing.

He tried to take a deep breath and calm his anger, knowing that she was safe now. It would have to be enough for now. A shot of jealousy went through him at the thought of Troy and Taby and their connection to her. It made him insane thinking how she had only calmed once they had said it was okay. That she trusted them and not him, but he would show her.

He didn't have a plan yet. It was something that he never did, going in without a detailed plan of action, but this time he was flying by the seat of his pants. His head was spinning with ideas on how to keep her close, but also to give her the space she needed. He could put a man on her so that he wasn't following her around all the time.

He would slowly introduce her to who he really was. He would work on her heart and body, drawing her closer to him till she was as obsessed as he was. He couldn't wait to get her under him and in a bed. Her curvy body was built like an angel, just for

51

him. Curving in a delicate line, making his hands itch to run along the lines of her.

The feelings she invoked within him were foreign and odd for him, but also empowering. He also felt a great dose of fear as well. If anyone was to find out how much she had come to mean to him. He shuddered at the thought. He had to protect her and everything she meant for him. She grounded him, even if she didn't know it. Just thinking of her seemed to pull him back from the blank shell of the person he never even knew he had become. She made him feel again, and for the first time he was looking forward to a future that he didn't even know he'd wanted.

One where work wasn't the center of his world. Where there was more than the seedy dealings of the men around him. The desires of the depraved.

The feelings that she gave him made him feel whole. Something he hadn't felt since before his mother died. Women for him had been something fleeting. There for a few hours or maybe days, before he would move on. Never wanting to build something more. Never wanting the connection. They served a purpose, and that was it.

So he did the only thing he could and watched her look out the window. He knew that, although his touch was still foreign to her, she had seemed receptive enough to him earlier. But he didn't want to push it. There would be time for that later. He had time; he wasn't letting her go. She just didn't know it yet.

The drive to the city was short and soon they were pulling up in front of his high rise. He got out first, helping her out after him, not willing to let anyone else help or touch her. He watched her shiver and realized that the thin shirt and sleep pants were not fit for her to be out in.

God, she doesn't even have shoes, he chastised himself. He would need to remedy that quickly. He was so concerned with getting her out of that rat-infested dump of a place she called home that he didn't think twice about her clothes.

He took off his jacket and placed it around her shoulders then hugged her close to his body, loving how she melted into him just a little. As she looked up at him, as if his kindness was something she wasn't used to, it made both his gut clench and his chest puff out in pride. He wanted her to have everything she wanted. He just wanted to be the only one that gave it to her.

The elevator pinged and the doors swooshed open for his floor. He urged her forward into the foyer and caught a shocked look on her face. He looked around the place, wondering how she saw it. She probably hadn't ever been in a place like this before.

He liked comfort but didn't know a thing about decorating, so he had hired someone. It was done in all black and white and had an open floor plan throughout the living room toward the back wall of windows and to the kitchen. On each side of the living room there were hallways leading off to bedrooms, and other rooms that he used as his office and for his security.

Looking toward her again he saw that what the place had been missing was her. Although the cold feel of the black and white never used to bother him, he now saw that it needed more. He needed a home that she would feel comfortable in. Thinking to himself of a way to change it, he decided to contact his secretary about it. She was a woman, so she would know.

"Come, are you hungry? Or do you want to go to bed?" he asked, taking off his jacket and laying it over the back of a large black leather sofa.

She hesitated, and he figured that she wasn't going to speak up to tell him what she needed. But as it was nearing five in the morning now, and she probably hadn't eaten the night before, he knew that she needed to eat something. As if on cue her stomach growled. She blushed, letting her head drop, and he smiled, staring down at her for a moment, taking in the sight of her red cheeks before him.

"Come," he said as he walked into the kitchen. He pulled out the makings for a sandwich, which was about the best he could manage with his cooking skills, and watched her gaze travel around his home while he worked.

"Sweetheart, sit." She was standing in the middle of the room, looking lost. He needed her to sit and settle a bit so he could talk to her. He didn't like how unsettled she was. He wanted her happy here with him.

She's probably going to crash soon, he thought.

She nodded and walked toward him with hesitant steps. His eyes never left hers as she pulled out a chair and sat down. He placed the sandwich he had made along with a glass of milk in front of her, and after only a second of hesitation she tore into it without thought. It made him both angry that she seemed as if she wasn't going to get food again, and happy that he could provide her with something that she needed. She moaned around the last bite and looked as if she was contemplating licking the crumbs off the plate.

"I can make another one, sweetheart." She startled but shook her head. She was so jumpy.

"No. I'm sorry I'm being rude. That was wonderful." She still hadn't looked him in the eye, though, and he was almost desperate for her to at this point. This all-consuming need when it came to her was new for him, but he wasn't going to stop and evaluate his feelings. He was who he was. And he was a man who always got what he wanted.

"Hey, look at me." He made sure to measure his tone so that she wouldn't be frightened.

Her beautiful eyes shot to him and he felt it in his gut. They were an unusual shade of brown, more like a caramel color with swirls that he could easily get lost in. As he gazed at her he hoped that she could see that he was serious in what he was going to say next. With her big wavy curls cascading down her back, she was a potent combination. She even had a few freckles on her nose.

"You will never again go hungry." It was a statement. He wouldn't accept anything else. Reaching out he cupped her jaw and leaned forward, placing his lips gently against her forehead. Letting the small contact wash over him, he knew that it was never going to be enough. Her touch. Her smell. Just her. He would never get enough.

She leaned into his touch as she closed her eyes, and it made his heart and dick clench. He could only hope that she felt the same way.

Chapter 9

Boris Stanley knew that he was likely not going to live a long life. He may not actually be a part of the West Coast Crime Syndicate or the local Familia, but his businesses were a direct part of them. He liked it that way. He could come and go as he pleased. Never committing to one person. It made for more money, too. That was the best, more money. More money led to more power, and more power gave him what he wanted.

Everything had been going well till Ivanov had asked him to acquire this new restaurant. He had needed a new location that was well between the Familia territory that he was taking over, and what Ivanov already had in territory. Boris worked a lot with Ivanov, and although he had no ties to one person, he did profit the most from him.

This new location was supposed to be a meeting place for Ivanov that was off the books, while providing him with another money source. He had planned to do away with all the staff and bring on his own people. People that he could either trust or manipulate. Sara was one of them.

A little coke on the side and she was as loyal to him as anyone. He snickered at the thought. She'd made herself very useful over the years. The bitch loved being in control of the bedroom, and he had a few people who had needed a good lesson. The fact that he often got to watch was only a bonus.

But nothing had gone to plan. With the contract for the new restaurant, he had to keep the old staff on. Most had left with only a few warnings, making it so he didn't have to worry about them. The few that stayed were a big pain. He couldn't risk firing them. They could report him. The one person that he hadn't minded staying was Alice.

She was a temptation of the worst sort. Her big eyes and well-placed curves were begging him to fuck her. With Sara's help, he had almost had her where he needed her—terrified and in need of keeping her job. He knew that she was trying to get through school. His plans were now dashed, though.

It had become a habit of his to watch the back room in secret. Silently peeking through one of the back doors, had given him lots of useful information over the last few months. When he saw Dominic's outburst and watched as he threw the glass against the wall, he knew it was time to leave. He didn't know where that little slut had run off to, but he hadn't waited to find out.

He walked out, got into his car, and drove away. If he made it home, he could grab some clothes and the money from his safe, and he would be home free. He had money stashed all over the world. He could disappear. It galled him to know that he would never get his hands on that little bitch, but his life was more important.

He parked his car and quickly made his way to his apartment door, his mind on what he needed to grab. He was so occupied that he didn't see the two men step out from beside the stairwell until it was too late. His fear overtook him at the look on their faces. He didn't think he was going to make it out of this.

Chapter 10

She woke up slowly. Feelings of warmth surrounded her, so comfy that she snuggled down into the billowing sheet around her. She paused at that, thinking that it was odd because her bed was never this warm. She blinked her eyes open to see a room of black and white illuminated by the sun coming through the windows. Where was she? She went to sit up and gasped as fiery pain shot through her hand, immediately remembering the night before.

Work, running from Dominic, and then him coming for her. He had brought her to his house, fed her, changed the bandage on her hand, and put her to bed.

It had been the most luxurious sleep she had ever had. It was only made stronger by the feelings of care that he had given her. She was a teen when her parents died, and she often forgot about what life was like with them in the face of what she dealt with every day.

She looked around the room, wondering what she should do. She figured that a shower was a good place to start, and then she would have to find some clothes. She was still in her nightclothes from the night before.

After a shower and putting on the clothes from yesterday, because she couldn't even find a robe in the room, she made her way downstairs. She could smell coffee, but she couldn't hear anyone. And after a small search around the room, she couldn't find anyone either.

She went in search of a mug after and filled one with the coffee that was already brewed and grabbed an apple from the bowl on the counter. She sat down at the table, staring out the window at the city. It was sunny and bright, giving the appearance of a warm day even though it was probably only thirty or forty degrees. She would need to figure out how to get a winter coat before too long.

Her mind wandered, making plans about what to do and where to go. She needed to get home and get a resume going. Dominic had said she was staying with him last night, but she knew better than to think that it would be a long-term solution. That was crazy! Besides, she could only count on herself. She doubted that she had a job after last night, and while she was relieved she no longer had to deal with Boris, it was going to be tough making rent and paying her bills, not to mention trying to get food. But she only had one semester left. She could do this. If she couldn't find a job soon, she knew that she could stay with Taby. Although she *really* didn't want to put her friend in that position, it was better than working for Boris. She was startled by a man walking into the kitchen.

"He would like to speak with you," the man said, a look on his face that she didn't particularly like. He seemed to be sneering at her, but she nodded and followed him, not wanting to rock the boat just yet. The man led her down the opposite hall that her room had been in, to a set of double doors.

Hesitantly walking in while keeping an eye on the scary man she first saw Dominic sitting behind his desk, engrossed in something. The door shut behind her, leaving her standing there wondering what to do. Dominic had yet to look up at her, and she could feel the stare of the other man behind her. She risked a glance at him and saw the same look as before. She thought that maybe it was disgust, so she decided to try and stay away from him.

"Alice." His command had her turning to see that he had already risen and was coming toward her. She wasn't sure what to expect this morning, but it wasn't the embracing hug that he gave her. Or the way that he led her over to the sofa and sat down, bringing her down on his lap. She glanced up to see the man frowning at them.

"You may go, Geo," Dominic said without looking away from her. Geo nodded and slipped out. She wanted to ask what his deal was, but thought better of it.

"You and I need to have a little talk," he said, cupping her jaw and holding her gaze on him. She was intrigued that he liked to always have her attention on him. It was different to feel this way. To have someone so devoted to her every move, and it unsettled her even more that she felt that way.

She could do nothing but nod at his statement. She was feeling out of her element, and figured that hearing him out wouldn't hurt anything. Then she could be on her way back home.

He seemed to be trying to think of how to start before he said, "I need you to understand some things before you answer my questions, okay?" At her nod, he continued.

"I realize that I'm moving very fast, but I also know how I feel. I want you to stay here." She tried to jerk out of his hold, but he tightened and then continued.

61

"Just hear me out. I want so much with you, sweetheart, stuff that I didn't even know was possible. A *real* life." He paused to gather himself before adding, "I want you to be mine. Just mine. In every way." His voice held none of the anger from yesterday at the restaurant and all of the hope and longing that she had often had after her parents had passed. It made her want those things, too, even if she knew better.

"But I know that you need your space. I know that I can't push you like I'm used to." He continued, "You can have your own room, your own space, till you're used to me. We can date and get to know each other. I don't want to cage you, but I just need you close."

She knew that she shouldn't consider his proposal but, amazingly, she was. This was the only time that she had felt safe, and right now she wanted to keep that feeling.

She had never felt like this with anyone else. Even with Taby and Troy, she held back. Not showing everything that was completely her. But with Dominic, she felt as if she could let go. That he would take care of everything. It was what she so desperately needed but was terrified to take. What if he turned out to be like her uncle? What if he got tired of her, where would she go then? But even with those terrifying thoughts she still couldn't shake the feeling that maybe this was where she was supposed to be.

"There are a few things that I need, though, that I can't bend on. I want monogamy. I will not share you." His voice was harder, his body tense under her till she nodded.

"You will get it from me as well." She felt a little more tension leave her body and she leaned into him. He seemed pleased by that, and his arms wrapped a little tighter around her as he kissed her forehead again. She felt her heart in her throat at such a simple gesture that gave her a feeling that she hadn't ever felt before. Whatever it was, it mixed with the desire that she felt for him.

She was glad that he had brought up monogamy. She knew that she wouldn't have even thought of staying if that hadn't been the case. Not only was she not that kind of girl, but knowing he was with another woman would break her. She hardly knew him, only spending a small amount of time around him, and yet she was already drawn to him. It was a scary and thrilling feeling.

"You will also have a security team with you. A lot is going on with my busines and family right now, and not all of it is ... well, I just need you to be safe." She wasn't sure how she felt about that. Having people follow her around. How would that work when she was working? And how would it work with school?

As much as she wanted to accept his offer, she didn't think she could do this. She needed to finish college, and even though she was close to being done, it still meant that she needed a job, that she would be gone a lot. Her shoulders slumped as she realized that a man like him could have anybody and that he wouldn't settle for the little bit of time that she could give him between classes and working. It just wasn't fair to him.

"My school ..." She trailed off, not knowing how to communicate what she needed to say.

"You will still have school," he interrupted, surprising her. "I wouldn't take that away from you. All I ask is that you have security with you at all times. You can have a life, Alice. I don't want to stop you. I just want to help; I want to be there with you along the way."

Her chest was near bursting, she didn't know she could feel this full. She knew it was ridiculous; this type of thing only happened in books and movies. Then she thought of her parents and the way they had loved each other.

Somehow, she knew that if she didn't accept his offer she would always regret it, whether it was a bad idea or not. She was tired of doing everything on her own. Tired of not having anybody there. Yes, she had Taby and Troy, but they were busy with their own lives. Besides, he had said that he would give her space. She could use that time to get to know him and still concentrate on school and finding another job.

She nodded shyly and he seemed to relax as if a weight had been taken off his shoulders, making her happy to have been the one to give that to him.

"Good. Because I wouldn't have accepted anything else," he said it with such an air of authority, that she chuckled. She could see him never stopping till he got what he wanted. It should have terrified her, but the sense of dread and fear didn't come like normal

"I love that sound." She didn't have time to process his sweet words as the hand holding her cheek slid around her neck and pulled her to him.

His lips landed on hers for a kiss. It wasn't just a kiss, though. It was sizzling, branding her from the inside out. Her world spun around her as he ate at her lips with teasing bites, his hand on her neck holding her in place for him, kneading. A small moan escaped her and she reached up and grasped his shoulders as she let herself sink into the feelings that he evoked in her.

After a time he stopped kissing her and drew back, leaving his hands around her neck possessively, holding her on his lap. She was dazed after their kiss and could feel him under her. Hard. She just barely resisted the urge to wiggle into him.

"Let me introduce you to your security," he said quietly in her ear, and motioned for her to get off.

"You already have someone?" she asked wondering how he worked that fast.

"Like I said, I wasn't going to let you say no."

They walked out to the main room where there was a group of men waiting. Two looked almost identical and she recognized them from the night before. The last was the man who had shown her to Dom's office. He had an angry look on his face. Geo, she remembered his name was. Based on his glare toward her, she hoped that he wasn't one that Dom had picked.

But her hopes were dashed when Dom introduced them. Dominic introduced as Rick and Danny, but her thoughts were scattered as Dominic started talking about her schedule. She realized that he knew a lot about it, more than she knew he did. She would have to ask him about that later. Glancing to her side, she watched as Geo's face became a mask of rage and she took a slight step back. Dominic must have felt it, because he looked back toward her.

"What?" he asked puzzled, not in tune with the rage focused on her.

She didn't know how to answer. These were his men— did she have the authority to question him in front of them? She didn't think it was a good idea. They were new and didn't know a lot about each other, but she didn't want to disrespect him, even unintentionally.

She glanced at him and slightly shook her head, indicating that she didn't want to talk right now. He frowned at

65

her but turned around and nodded at each of the men, then walked her back tohis office, dragging her behind him.

"Talk," he demanded once they were alone. He stepped back from her and crossed his arms over his chest. He seemed very upset that she hadn't given him an answer.

"Geo seemed upset," she told him, now that they didn't have an audience. He tilted his head and frowned as if he was trying to figure something out, looking so confused, and she giggled.

"I want to hear more of that," he said quietly, a small quirk to his lips showing. The tension gone now, she stepped into him as he wrapped his arms around her. Slowly his head bent and he kissed her. This one was softer than the first kiss but no less passionate, and by the time he pulled away she was practically a puddle on the floor. The man could kiss.

He stepped back from her, saying, "I didn't have time to get someone to come fit you for clothes, so online will have to work. I put a few things in the cart." He gestured toward his computer. "But you will need to add more to it. We will get that done now, and your stuff will be delivered by this afternoon. You won't be going to classes today, but security will be set up for you tomorrow." She could tell a difference in him already—he was in business mode. She recognized his attitude change from the few meetings at the restaurant.

She thought for a moment and realized that there was probably a lot that he didn't show people in his business world.

It made her wonder what side of the man she would get.

For instance, he was telling her what to do and not asking. Deciding not to say anything, she knew that it was going to take some time to get to know each other. Only time would tell if she could trust him to speak her mind.

Better to wait it out, she thought.

"Now let's rewrap your hand," he said, leading her away.

Chapter 11

Two Weeks Later

She sat in the living room, staring at her new phone as she and Taby messaged back and forth, even though she had just gotten back from having lunch with her. It had been wonderful to see her and have some time that wasn't filled with work or school. With everything going on with Taby and Troy moving, and now that they didn't work together, it had been the first time that they had seen each other and not just talked on the phone.

She had needed the time too. To get a chance to talk to Taby face to face. Everything was happening so fast that she had whiplash from it all. Taby hadn't seemed worried about it and just told her not to worry, that she was there if she needed her. She also hinted that she thought that Dominic taking care of her was a good thing.

"Sweetie, you have always, since I've known you, been on your own. You have a wall around you that even I can't get through. It's not a bad thing to have someone take care of you"—she paused, then added in a very exaggerated Taby manner—"especially if he's hot."

She was unused to someone taking care of her, and it felt odd to not have to worry about everything. But she didn't like to think of herself as closed off. However, with her past, she knew that she held some stuff back. She felt as if this whole experience with Dominic was all a dream, one that she really hoped was real.

One bright spot were Danny and Rick being on her security. They had seemed genuine and they were hilarious. They instantly put her at ease once Dominic had left. Geo hadn't softened toward her at all and had stood in the room, glaring at her. She had tried to not let it affect her. That was what he was doing now. She was about to make her excuses and go to her room when the elevator dinged. The Danny and Rick stood as Geo went to let in whoever it was.

She still wasn't used to this level of security, and it was almost frightening. She was given a list by Geo of all the things she could and couldn't do. She had to inform them when she wanted to go somewhere at a certain time. And she couldn't answer the elevator. Honestly, the list of things she couldn't do was enormous. It made school a bit of trouble going from class to class, not to mention trying to find a job. One place had refused to accept her application with Geo standing behind her.

She wondered why any man would need this much security, but figured it was something to do with his job. Something that she hadn't asked about yet, but she had a suspicion. Of course, there was Taby and her gossip about Dominic. But everyone knew who the Mancini family was. It only made sense, she just didn't know how he was a part of it.

A tall, thin woman dressed in a sleek dressy business suit walked in, following another person who was pushing a kind of rolling clothing rack. The colors and designs on it made her cringe. They were bright and full of fabrics that looked as if they were as stiff as a board.

Definitely not jeans. This was not what she would have picked at all. Dominic had been buying clothes for her left and right. She had so far been able to put him off with only a few things here and there, but she knew he was done with that when he announced that a designer would be coming, and if she didn't pick enough he would. The look on his face made her think that it would not be the simple jeans and t-shirts that she would have picked out.

The woman paused and looked at her with a sneer worse than Geo's, then turned.

"You're right she needs a lot of work. Why in the world would he pick … that?" She finished with a wave and a flourish toward her.

Alice's face went pink in embarrassment. She knew that she probably wasn't what Dominic normally would go for in a woman. Someone sleek and suave. Probably someone like the woman standing in front of her. But she was who she was and Dominic didn't seem to mind. On the other hand, he had to know that these were not her types of clothes. Was he trying to change her? At that thought, she looked over to Geo and saw him smirking in her direction.

The man really didn't like her, she thought.

"Hey! Watch your mouth!" Rick shouted as both he and Danny came up behind her. They both had been on edge with Geo's attitude with her, but as far as she knew they hadn't said anything to Dominic. There was a hierarchy that Danny had explained to her. Geo was Dominic's second and head of security, then Danny and Rick followed. She got the impression that it wasn't their place to interfere.

"But Mr. Dominic loves my mouth." The woman smirked, her meaning clear, and Alice could feel the blood drain from her face. This woman had been with Dominic? And he had brought her here? Danny and Rick both made a move toward the woman when Geo spoke up.

"That's enough. She's allowed to speak her mind. Dom's had plenty of whores here before. You two go finish up the books in the back." The last was said to Danny and Rick, but she didn't notice them leave. She was replaying Geo's words in her head, and if she could have gone any paler she would have as her stomach plummeted. Was that what Dominic thought of her? What everyone thought of her? Was that why he brought her here?

"I'm tired. I'm sorry, but I'm not feeling up to this right now," she murmured as she fled the room. She could hear the Danny and Rick yelling at Geo behind her and ran faster, not wanting to be a part of it.

Did Dominic really think of her like that? She had thought that he had wanted to start a relationship with her. When he looked at her she felt as if he was trying to speak right to her soul. She felt it. She felt him. And she felt safe.

These last couple of weeks have been nothing but the best times that she had had since her parents. He wasn't home often, but when he did come home he came straight to her. They talked about their days, and she felt as if he cared. But was it worth it if they weren't building something? He hadn't made a move to take her to bed yet, but she knew that he was turned on. She could see the desire in his eyes every time he looked at her. Could feel it when he was holding her. But a whore? The whole thing was a big, jumbled mess, and she didn't know what to think.

Those words kept replaying in her mind. If everything Geo had said was true, then she was no better off than when she was with her uncle.

It was too good to be true, she thought. No matter how much she had hoped otherwise.

Geo reminded her of her uncle when he looked at her. Like she was dirt on the bottom of his shoe. Her uncle had never actually touched her sexually, only threatened her with it, but he had become good at using his fists. When he was beating her he had always talked about how the only reason he was keeping her around was that he was going to make money off her. He had liked to call her his high roller.

She wasn't naive like most people thought. Just because she was quiet didn't mean she didn't listen. She knew that her uncle was a bad man and that he sold women and drugs. It's why she had run; she didn't want anything to do with it.

Should she try to leave again? Even if she could, she was still in her PJs and had no money. She had her bus pass, but she couldn't go traipsing around the city without a coat or shoes. And besides, she didn't know how to work the elevator. She would have to wait for Dom to come home. Then he could take her to Taby's. She couldn't stay here. Not if that was what people saw her as.

***

Four days later she was still there, wondering if she had made the right choice. She knew that she should have left that first night after that woman and Geo talked about her like that, but she had wanted to give Dominic a chance.

He had come home that night and calmed all of her fears. That he had never been with her, Melissa he said her name was, and that Geo was just stressed with a business merger that they were dealing with right now.

That he was with her now, and that it would take time for her to settle in. Then he had kissed her forehead and tucked her into bed. She had felt cherished even as a little part of her thought that he was ignoring her, and only saying what she wanted to hear.

Melissa had left the clothes in the apartment. She had put them away in the closet and saw that none of them would fit right, and even if they did, they were gaudy and horrible. Something that a woman on the arm of a man like Dominic would wear, she guessed. But honestly, she couldn't see Dominic liking any of these either.

She had called Taby, who had promised to bring her some jeans and a sweatshirt to school the next day. Her possessions had come, but it was only her school stuff and a few pictures that she had. Her clothes and everything else they had left at her old apartment. The thought made her sad that her life could be put into one or two boxes. Not even large boxes at that.

The next day Taby tried reassuring her. She tried telling her that Dominic was going through some stuff with his businesses and it was probably just a misunderstanding. She had tried to listen to her, but at night when she went to bed before he came back she still was plagued with fears of what was really going on.

Now it was Wednesday and her day off from school. So she had spent the first half of the day on her homework, and she hoped that this afternoon she could go drop off a couple more applications.

Sitting on the couch, trying not to think about Dominic and how lonely she was, the emptiness of it all started to get to her. Why had he brought her here if he was just going to leave her? What was the point?

He was never home, and when he was he seemed preoccupied. She understood that he had a lot going on, but she deserved better than how he was treating her. She had given him a chance and risked herself and her heart for him, and he didn't seem to care at all. She had stupidly believed that she had a reason to believe in the hope that he was offering.

Her mind swirled with her thoughts the whole day, till she found herself sitting on the couch watching the news after eating another dinner by herself. She was stewing in her head when the screen flashed an image of a big charity party. She couldn't believe what she was seeing.

There was Dominic dressed very handsome in a black tux, his hair perfectly done as he faced the cameras. And there on his arm was Melissa. Her blonde hair was done up, leaving her neck and chest and back exposed, a deep blue dress hugging her every curve. She felt sick.

"Fuck," muttered Rick, sitting next to her. It was one of the rare times that Geo wasn't there and so the Danny had been trying to lighten the mood and cheer her up.

"Um, Alice ..." he began, but she didn't care what he was going to say. She fled before the tears could come. Running down the hall and slamming the door shut, she flung herself onto the bed. She could hear Rick and Danny calling to her through the door, but she had only one thought in her head.

Geo had been right.

She knew then that it wasn't going to work. That she needed to leave. She just needed to figure out how.

Chapter 12

The next morning didn't make it any easier on her. After a restless night where Dominic had never come back, she had concluded that it no longer mattered what he would say. She needed to leave. She texted Taby, asking if she could stay with them, then she had packed what little she could take in her school bag as she got ready to go.

Walking out of her room, though, she realized that she forgot to give Geo her schedule for her finals. She had been so preoccupied trying to pack her stuff up while her heart felt like it was cracking inside.

"Sorry, you didn't tell me earlier. Can't." His tone and look said that he wasn't sorry at all.

Danny and Rick were both frowning at him from across the table, but she had learned enough to know that Geo was their boss and they couldn't really stand up to him, even if they wanted to. She wondered if Dominic knew about how Geo treated her or if he just didn't care.

"But it's my final," she pleaded, but he just shrugged and went back to reading his paper. She was sick of this. What did she do to deserve this?

She squared her shoulders, *she would not miss her finals*, she thought. They meant too much, and when she was done, she certainly wasn't coming back here.

She walked back to her bedroom, leaving the door open. If she wanted a chance at the elevator she needed them all out of the front room. Half an hour later she was wondering if she was going to miss her finals, when the men finally walked off down the opposite hall toward Dominic's office.

She listened to make sure that they weren't coming back then, with her coat on and carrying her shoes so as not to make any noise, she crept down the hall and to the front. Next to the elevator door was a panel that had an intercom system and security panel. She had seen Danny enter his code just yesterday and had memorized it, knowing that she might need it.

As quickly as she could she entered the code. The doors slid open and she clambered inside, hitting the button for the ground floor. The door swishing closed behind her, but she didn't relax. There was only a small amount of time that she would be able to pull this off. Putting on her shoes, she could only hope that she made it before they caught her.

The bell dinged for every floor, adding to her nerves. And by the time it hit the ground floor she was wringing her hands and half scared out of her mind.

She didn't think that Dominic would physically hurt her, but she wasn't willing to find out. She knew for sure, though, that after that first night in his office he would not let her go easily. This was the only way.

76

The doors swooshed open and she ran out the front door and down the street, and straight to the first bus stop she came across. Luck was with her as it was one with a bus just pulling up. Finding a seat she sat with a great heaving laugh. Ha! She had done it.

She smiled big at the thought, looking over her shoulder and out the back of the window. She was out. She checked the time on her watch.

She had just enough time to make it to her final.

***

Dominic had had it. It had been four days, and it wasn't getting any better. The reports about Alice, from Geo, weren't looking good, and then she had turned him down for the gala. The thought still pissed him off. He had shown up to that damn charity event, thinking that he would finally get to spend some time with her. Only to have Geo's sister, Melissa shoved in his face.

At first, he tried to give her the space she needed. He could at least act like a civilized person and try to not run her over. He was overbearing on the best of days, and most of the time he liked it like that. He liked being in control. However, he figured she probably needed a day to get her head wrapped around everything. He had lost his patience after a few weeks though, enough was enough!

He had tried to stay with her for the first few days and work from home, but eventually he had to go to work. His clubs had gone without him for so long that the list of things he needed to do was as long as his arm. The first time he had to leave for the full day hadn't been until after a couple of weeks. He had tried reassuring himself that she was getting a spa day and her fitting for her clothes.

That night she had spouted some stuff that he hadn't paid half attention to, as tired as he was and just tried to reassure her. It had been about his past with some woman and, honestly, he hadn't known what to say. She knew that he had a past. They both did. He didn't need it thrown in his face all the time. He had tried to tell her that she was the only woman in his life then went to bed, passing out before his head even hit the pillow.

What he had not counted on was the time that he wasn't going to have. This week was the merger of his club over to Ivanov. Along with giving up his position with the Familia, he also had to sign over two of his clubs. Something that he was happy to do if it got him out and fulfilled his grandfather's wish. But the amount of time it was consuming was getting to him.

He normally tried to only go to the office a couple of times a week, he had a whole building of people that did the work for him after all, but this week had been crazy. He had to be there to sign forms and attend meetings, and for the last two days he hadn't even made it home. Just slept in his office.

A first for him and something that he hoped would be a last. He missed her with a depth that he didn't know he possessed and had been looking forward to seeing her at the charity gala. But Geo had said she gave some half-assed excuse and didn't want to come.

Didn't want to.

Why the hell not?

So yes ... he was pissed.

The phone ringing brought him out of his thoughts and he considered letting it go because, honest to God, all he wanted to do was go home and see what her problem was. But he couldn't. It was his personal phone and that meant it was important.

Flipping it open without looking to see who it was, he answered, "What!"

"Boss, we got a problem." It was Rick, and at the same instant he spoke his desk phone started ringing but he ignored it.

"Listen to me okay? Something's up with Geo. Your girl, man it's bad. Fuck, I don't know all that's going on between you two, but she saw the news feed last night. Saw you with Melissa. And Geo's been saying stuff. Fuck, I don't know." Rick seemed distracted and worried, and he gritted his teeth, just wanting answers.

"What the hell are you talking about!" His patience was running thin and Rick wasn't making any sense. And why the hell was Rick calling him and not Geo!

"I don't care what she is to you, man, but you can't fuckin' treat her like this." The click of dead air left him with more questions than answers.

His desk phone rang again and he quickly picked it up. This time it was Geo.

"What the hell is going on?" he yelled.

"The girl fucking ran! She snuck out. She's gone. She was saying all this crap about how you didn't come home to her and such bullshit. And I don't know, man, she's gone." Geo kept rambling but Dominic didn't listen. He didn't think. Slamming the phone down, he grabbed his keys and ran for his car.

He knew where she was going to be. The girl thought that she could play games. That she could leave.

He had told her that he wouldn't take no for an answer.

He was done giving her space.

Chapter 13

She had done it. She had finished the semester. She should be happy but even the thought of being done couldn't completely wipe away all that had happened today. She had done the right thing by leaving and not letting herself be treated that way again. But that didn't mean she was thrilled with the idea of having no job and no place to live. Not to mention her heart hurt at the thought of never seeing Dominic again.

Taby was sitting across from her at a table in the library as they waited for Troy to pick them up. Alice had just finished telling Taby all that had gone on this morning and she was pissed. Taby was always overdramatic, but when she was mad she was a force to be reckoned with. She often wondered how Troy even dealt with her.

"God!" Taby yelled, causing some of the students a row over to look at them.

"I can't believe it. I thought he was going to be good for you. Troy and I talked about him and how he wanted you, would take care of *you* for once." She was flailing her arms around as she spoke and it made Alice smile, watching her. No matter how crazy she got, she really did love her and how fierce she was for her benefit.

"How does Troy know him?" She was curious as to how two different areas of her life had ended up overlapping.

"They were childhood friends, I guess. Grew up down the street together. Troy's foster family let him just roam, and I guess he hung out over there a lot. When they got older Dominic was busy, but they still kept in touch. Dominic was the one that paid for Troy's attorney, I guess. Troy says that he's the only real family he's got even if they don't keep in touch all that much." Alice thought about that.

She knew that neither Troy nor Taby had any real family with them just like her. She hated that she might be creating a rift between them.

"God! I can't believe him!" Taby shouted again, this time also stomping her foot.

"Taby, it's fine. I just need …" She paused, embarrassed at having to ask for help but having no choice.

"I need a place to stay." She went into more detail about how he had moved her out of her apartment and thrown out all her stuff with it. She hadn't been that mad about it at the time, but now that she knew she couldn't count on him she was. She wouldn't even have a bed to put in an apartment when she could find one. Of course, that was after she found a job.

"Yes! You don't even have to ask. UGH! Troy is going to be so pissed."

They talked for a while longer till Troy texted Taby, saying that he was out front waiting for them. To her dismay, though, when they walked out the front doors she saw that he wasn't alone.

She should have realized that Dominic would come after her, and she didn't know why she didn't think of it. She had been so concerned with just getting out of his apartment that she hadn't thought beyond that.

Worse, Geo was with him.

They were standing there, along with Rick and Danny, all talking with Troy. Together they made quite the formidable group, and she was sure that everyone on campus was staring at them.

She wasn't sure what she was going to say, but the look on his face was terrifying. It brought her back to his outburst in the restaurant. Reminding her that she wasn't really safe at all. Her hands grew clammy and her breathing grew more frantic at the thought of the coming confrontation. All her earlier bravado left her. Taby, sensing her distress, grabbed her hand, squeezed in reassurance, then dragged her along and marched right up to Dominic.

"How dare you!" Taby screamed at Dominic, poking a finger out toward him. "You convinced me that you were going to be good for her. You worked all along so you could get her out of that restaurant, then you discard her and have her thinking she's only there for a personal booty call!"

Alice's face went pink as Taby blurted out what was going on and she dropped her eyes, not wanting to see the reactions of anybody. They had drawn quite a crowd and she was wishing a hole would open up and swallow her.

"What did you say?" Dom's voice was deceptively calm and quiet, menacing. A voice that would scare anybody else. Troy stepped forward as if to stop Taby, or maybe protect her, but she knew that Taby was on a roll. Maybe it was because Troy was there, maybe it was because they were out in the open. But Taby didn't back down. Alice had never seen her stand up to anyone before like this before. Sure, she was a spunky person, but that was different than telling someone off.

"You heard me! How dare you think that you could do that to her! Well, guess what? It's done! I'm not letting anyone treat her like that. Even you!" That last was screamed, and several things happened at once.

Troy reached for Taby at the same time that Geo pulled out his gun, shouting, "Shut that bitch's mouth!" And Dominic went for her.

Her body was frozen at the terrifying look on his face, but the Danny and Rick were faster and in the blink of an eye, they had dragged her back and stepped in front of her. Dominic skidded to a halt, staring at them in outrage, fury covering his face.

"You mean to keep me from what's mine?!" His voice sent a wave of rage over all of them, hitting her fully, sending chills. People took off running at the menacing thunder of his voice. Her body was shaking, a fresh wave of fear broke out. This was going all wrong, and she figured that soon the cops would be here.

"She's mine!" he roared, looking like he was about to lose it. She caught Geo's face, standing behind Dom, and saw the evil glint in his eyes and wondered how much of this was his doing. She glanced over to Troy who was way back at the car with Taby, who was wriggling and yelling out her name, trying to get to her.

"Boss. We are doing our job. We are protecting her. Stand down, man." Danny spoke in a firm tone. Rick wrapped his arm back behind himself and patted her hip in reassurance.

She looked up to see Dom's face blanketed in shock. Her heart hurt looking at him. He was the image of everything that she thought was going right, only to be ripped out from under her again.

The sound of sirens came from the distance and all the men flew into action. Danny grabbed her arm and ran for a car with Rick climbing into the driver's seat. She briefly saw Troy take off with Taby, and she was glad to know that she was going to be safe, even if her own future was shaky at best.

She knew that she could always count on Taby and Troy, but now knowing their past and connection with Dominic she didn't know if she could involve them.

Danny pushed her into the back of the town car, coming in after her, with Dominic flying in after him. She shrank back in her seat, away from Dominic as much as possible, and saw him frown at her. His body was still tense and rigid, his suit impeccable as always, his hair hanging over his face again. A wave of sadness went through her, thinking that he wasn't *really* hers anymore.

Rick drove away quickly, passing the police that drove in, headed in the opposite direction of them. Danny and Dominic's heads were turning back and forth, watching for any sign that they were being followed by the cops.

Their reaction to the sounds of the sirens scared her, and she had the thought again of his connections to the local Mafia.

Maybe Taby was right, she thought.

Chapter 14

"Clear!" Rick called from the front, and both Dominic and Danny seemed to relax some.

Danny took a big breath and ran his hand through his hair. He reached forward and grabbed a water bottle, offering it to her. She just shook her head. She didn't think that it would stay down right now. Her nerves were shot, and her stomach was doing flips. This whole thing was too much. She couldn't take much more. Danny frowned at her but didn't say anything.

"Can someone tell me what the hell is going on?" Dominic finally spoke up, his voice betraying that his patience was gone. He was always so controlled she knew that to push him this far, it couldn't be good. Though he didn't yell, she thought, so that was probably a bonus.

"And why the hell did you run?" he accused, turning an angry stare at her, but it was Danny that spoke.

"I let her go." Both she and Dominic turned toward him. She was astonished, Dominic frightening. That was news to her.

"I saw you leave, Alice. Knew that your final was today. Did you pass?" She nodded and he gave her a brief smile.

"What the hell is going on!" This was bellowed. She wrapped her arms around her knees, pulling back even farther into the seat, hoping that if he lashed out that Danny or Rick would protect her.

"Something's up with Geo," Rick said from the front, and Danny nodded in affirmation. Dom seemed to pause and consider their words. Then he turned to her.

"Why is it that you think I'm just using you for sex?" His voice had settled slightly and only held a little of the impatience from before. She still flinched when he spoke, and his lips tightened as he caught it. She looked to Danny, hoping that he would help her out, but he only gestured that she needed to do this part on her own.

He might be there to protect her, but right now she was on her own. When she started talking her words still came out soft at first, and gradually they gained momentum as her anger started to take over. A feeling she wasn't used to. Fear yes. Not anger.

"You think because I'm a waitress that I'm going to be happy with fancy clothes and waiting for you at home locked in my room. You think I will be happy enough with the time that you decided to grace me when you're not with your girlfriend." Dominic jerked, then frowned at her words. But she was on a roll now and it felt awesome to finally be able to have her say.

"Oh, I know all about your girl, Melissa, and her wonderful mouth," she said with as much sarcasm as she could muster, her hands making air quotes. "Well screw you, Dominic! You can take your girlfriend and shove it for all I care. Oh ... and your stinking rules, too! I wasn't going to miss my final just because you felt like I hadn't given you enough time or some bullshit. I—"

"That's enough," he said harshly. She stopped abruptly at his words, her chest heaving from yelling. She had been near shouting at the end. Danny was smiling wide at her and Rick was chuckling in the front seat.

She realized what she had done and her cheeks went pink. She had just yelled at Dominic. She hoped that he didn't lose his temper, but then she thought that even if he did it had been worth it.

"What rules?" Dominic questioned, his teeth grinding.

"Geo," Danny started to say, but a glare from Dominic along with a hand being held up stopped him.

"I want to hear from her." He gestured to Alice, and she felt that bravado leave her again.

"What rules?" he questioned again. His tone was calm, his face blank. And looking at him she saw that he had pulled back. Hiding behind the mask he had. *Maybe they were not that different*, she thought. Both of them hiding behind a front for others to see.

"The rules that I have to follow. When I can leave. Geo explained them all to me. He said that you needed me to follow them," she whispered, not understanding why she was having to explain all this. He was acting like he had no idea what was going on either.

Dominic stared at her with that blank look. But his dark eyes betrayed his emotion. They were glittering dangerously, and she knew why when he pulled out his phone and pushed a few buttons before bringing it to his ear. She could hear the ringing in the background. The longer it rang the angrier his face became. Finally, he ended the call and tried again.

"Find Geo." He hung up with a slam. "Pull over," Dominic said, and Rick put his blinker on and started to ease to the side of the road.

"Go up front." He gestured to Danny and when he hesitated Dominic reiterated, "Go up front. We need to talk."

She gulped, thinking that maybe she had gone too far. He seemed to be really upset about the whole mess, so what did that mean for her? After another second of hesitation, Danny nodded and left the back of the car. Rick drove away as soon as the door was shut.

Dominic reached forward and pressed a button that rolled the glass divider up between the two sections. She knew that cars like this existed, but she was still a little in awe of the luxury of it all. After the divider was rolled up, they sat in silence for a few minutes. She could tell that he was trying to calm down.

"I'm sorry," he said softly, and her eyes widened at his response. That wasn't what she had expected him to say at all. Getting up, he half crawled to the seat next to her. Using her moment of shock he pulled her onto his lap, stroking her hair.

"I have never said that to anybody else." She had figured that out, but the fact that he admitted to that told her just how important this whole thing was.

"Your reports said that …well, I'm guessing that it's all a crock of shit."

"Reports?" she asked quietly, figuring that she knew what he was talking about but wanting to know for sure.

"I was trying to give you space and not crowd you, also I've been so busy the last few days. So I had Geo let me know what was going on and how you were doing."

He was starting to look angry again and she wanted to calm him. She lifted her hand to his chest and his gaze flew to hers. He was as shocked as she was that she had done that.

"Why did you go to the thing ... you know, with her? With Melissa," she said softly, unable to keep the hurt out of her voice. She needed to know why he had treated her like that.

"It was a mistake, baby. Geo said that you didn't want to go, and then she showed up in that dress." His hands clenched on her hip.

"What does the dress have to do with any of this? I know she looked beautiful in it. Is that your excuse for sleeping with her?" she said heatedly, trying to shove her way off his lap, no longer wanting to be near him. At her words, his face broke out in a full smile, making her even madder.

"This is not funny!" He started laughing in earnest, and she felt the urge to hit him.

"I like it when your claws come out. It lets me know that the real you is in there and that maybe you might want me just a fraction of the amount that I need you." He ended his words with a kiss on her forehead.

"The dress I picked out for you was a surprise. I wanted to see you in the dark blue, draped over your body. God. I knew you would look beautiful in it." He shook his head, as desire washed over his face, making her shiver, momentarily forgetting where and what she was doing. The feeling of him washed over her. His face drooped, anger returning as he continued.

"Then Geo told me that you didn't want to come and that you didn't want to wear it." He frowned. "And I didn't sleep with her." She wanted so badly to believe him, but she didn't know if she should.

"I never got it, Dominic. I never even knew that you wanted me to go. The first I heard of it was when I saw you on TV."

He nodded as if he knew this. Was this really just a big mistake? She needed to be brave and ask. She was starting to believe that he wouldn't ever hurt her physically, she just needed to make sure that he wasn't going to hurt her emotionally.

But before she could ask him, he cupped her face in his hands. He didn't bring her in any closer, he just stared deep into her eyes.

"A lot is going on that I can't tell you, but just know that Geo will never hurt you again." His eyes were burning bright with emotion, and she knew that he was feeling the connection between them. Desire and need like a string between them.

He drew her forward and nibbled on her lips. She should protest, to make him explain what had happened with everything that he wasn't telling her about, but she couldn't help how he made her feel.

So, she followed her heart and melted into him. Letting his kisses ease away the last few days. His hands started to wander to her waist, pulling her into him, and she started to feel the desire that he evoked in her rise to the surface. She moved, her leg swinging to straddle him, her hands at his neck. Moving together, his hands flexed on her waist as if holding himself back from pulling her down on to the hardness that she could feel under her.

They had never done more than just make out a few times, never going further than a few moments with wandering hands. Always stopping before their desire climbed too high. Not this time, though. She knew what she wanted.

Him.

Just him.

This time she didn't stop. She let go. Sitting back on his lap, feeling him tense as she rolled her hips slightly against the bulge in his pants.

"Fucking hell, sweetheart." His words grated over her skin, adding to the fire that consumed her as she held him, nipping and biting his lips, his hips now thrusting and grinding against her.

Lost in each other, nothing else mattered. She jumped back at the sudden knock on the divider window. His hands grasped her hips, not letting her leave his lap.

"Christ." He tipped his head back, eyes closed. Chest heaving, she watched him try to compose himself.

The image of him in front of her, the angles of his face, his broad shoulders. Strong. She nearly moaned at the thought of her hands on him, both of them twisted up in his sheets. She cleared her throat, reaching up to straighten her hair while trying to compose herself. She looked up at Dominic to see him grinning at her.

"What?"

"You look perfect."

"You mean I look like I just made out in the back of a car." She smirked.

"Exactly." She couldn't help but laugh at his answer.

His gaze turned serious.

"You have to promise not to run like that again." He held up a hand, silencing her when she would have spoken out.

"I know why you did it, but something like that will not happen again and I need you to understand that it isn't safe."

She understood the underlying message that he wasn't saying. His life wasn't always safe and she needed to let him take care of her, but she still would have done it for her school. She wasn't going to tell him that.

"I'm proud of you though, baby." His words shocked her, but before she could gather herself and ask him why he was getting out of the car and coming around to her door.

He helped her out of the car and into the high rise building that was slowly starting to become her home. They stepped into the elevator and he inserted his code to take him to the top. She watched in the mirror as he turned toward her, catching his eyes. His arms came up around her waist. One at her hip and one around her neck. His gaze seared straight through her as if he was searching for something, and dang if she didn't want to give it to him.

"I'm going to kiss you." His whispered words feathered over her skin.

Pulling her head to the side toward him, his lips pressed to hers. She gave herself over to the kiss and the feel of his lips on hers. His hands slid up into her hair, tilting her head and deepening the kiss. She moaned into his mouth as he deepened the kiss, their desire still on the edge from the car.

His tongue brushed along her lips and she felt the tingle through her whole body go up in flames of need, unlike anything she had ever felt. She moaned as his fingers flexed on her hip and he moved his body closer into her till they were flush from head to toe. His leg slid between her legs while he pulled her into him. Putting pressure exactly where she needed it, causing her to rock slightly against him. Searching for the high that only he would be able to give her. She heard a mewling sound and realized it was coming from her.

"Boss." The voice seemed far away but Dominic jerked, drawing his lips away from hers and looked over his shoulder, not moving his body away from her.

Protecting her.

She glanced around him and saw that they were on his floor and the elevator door was wide open. Both Danny and Rick were standing there with the biggest smiles on their faces.

"You want me to close the elevator doors, man?" How Danny said that without choking on his laughter was beyond her.

"Fuck," Dom whispered and stepped away from her, dragging her into the apartment, his frustration very apparent. The bulge in his pants gave him away.

Rick and Danny busted up laughing, their bodies shaking, as Dominic pulled her behind him, stomping by the men.

"Fuck you!" he said over his shoulder. She started laughing, too.

Chapter 15

Dinner was a quiet affair. He ordered Italian food from a little café down the street. She was thrilled of course; what girl didn't like a big bowl of pasta, especially after the day she had had. The low tones of the news on the TV in the background filled the silence as they ate.

As they ate the scene from the elevator and the car kept playing in her mind and she wondered what would have happened if they hadn't been interrupted. Dominic was definitely her kryptonite. He could make her forget everything and just drown in the feelings he evoked. For the first time she wondered if she could actually feel safe, that if she gave him everything she might have what her parents had had.

"Done?" His words brought her out of her inner thoughts and she nodded at him. He gathered up their trash and dishes while she went to turn the TV off.

They met in the hallway that led to the bedrooms and he grabbed her hand, leading her. When they stopped at her door he didn't let go of her hand. He twisted it and brought it up to his chest, still holding it with his as he moved his body into hers, pressing her into the door jamb. She watched as he bent his head and lightly brushed his lips across their joined hands. She let out a swoosh of air as his gaze connected with hers. His eyes were gleaming with a heat she had never experienced, and she could swear that she felt it clear to her toes.

She stood transfixed as he leaned closer and brushed his nose along hers. Her eyes fell closed as she took in the sensations.

His body pressed against hers.

His lips brushing against hers.

She was drowning in him.

She opened for him, hoping for more, and he obliged by deepening the kiss. Sliding one of his hands to wrap around her, rubbing along the edge of her shirt. She blindly moved back as he pushed and maneuvered them into her room and toward her bed.

He nipped her lip with his teeth and a moan left her as he grasped her shirt and brought it over her head. Quick as a flash he was back to kissing her and sliding his hands around her back and into her hair. Giving her no time to slow down, to think. Not that she wanted to. This feeling was like nothing she had ever felt before.

It was consuming.

It was empowering.

Her knees hit the bed as he backed her up to it and followed her down. Never stopping his onslaught of kisses.

Abruptly he pulled back, a moan of disappointment leaving her.

"Do you want this? We don't have to do this. I am just fine continuing as we have. I want you to trust me." He bent and gave her a brief and gentle kiss. Completely different than the hard set to his body.

"I need your trust," he whispered, as she reached up, grasping his neck and bringing him back to her. Looking into his eyes, she made a decision.

Whether she came to regret it later or not, she no longer cared. She was head over heels with him, falling hard. Dominic had come into her life and taken over. Wanting and accepting nothing less than all of her, even if it took forever he would wait. He didn't have to wait, though. She wanted this. She wanted what he was promising. No matter all that had happened, she would give this to him.

"I trust you. I'm yours." She watched her words flow over him. He captured her lips with a searing kiss.

Hard.

Demanding.

Branding.

Loving.

Everything.

He followed with small nibbles, enough to drive her mad.

"Yes, baby. You're mine." He returned her kisses and brought his hands up to her neck to hold her in place as his kisses increased.

The desire flowing through her made her squirm under him, desperate for some relief. But he wasn't giving it to her. Determined to only let her move to his will. He confirmed that a second later, whispering, "When you are in my bed, I'm in control. Your movements, your orgasms. They are mine." His words slid along her like his lips against her neck. "I promise if you give me that, give me you, you'll get all of me, baby. I promise."

Done with words, he kissed her. His hands trailed to her breast, twisting as she arched up into his passion. *It had never felt like that*, she thought. It was wonderful. His skilled hands twisted her nipples, leaving a pinch of pain then soothing relief. She was mindless by the time his hand trailed through her panties. To her folds where she was wet and waiting for him.

Every loss and touch he brushed against her skin left a trail of fire in its wake. Her breathing was uneven she felt his fingers twisting and sliding between her legs, and she realized that somehow he had gotten her panties off without her knowing.

How did he manage that?

Before she had time to answer herself or ask him how he had managed such a feat, his fingers brushed against her outer lips and straight against her clit. She jolted, arching at the pleasure of it. She had never had something feel that good; it just wasn't the same when she did it herself, and her limited sexual experiences were nothing compared to this. Her arms came up to wrap him up, grasping at his neck, desperate to get a hold of the emotions that were consuming her. His finger dipped lower and she moaned, arching her hips, searching for more.

"Fuck, baby!" he grunted out before his mouth crashed down on hers while his finger slid through that moisture and straight into her, leaving her breathless and shaking. His movements at first were slow and easy and she could feel the firestorm inside her as she flew higher and higher.

"Let go, baby. Give it to me. Fuck, yes," he grated out harshly against her neck, but she was so high she didn't hear him as she flew apart. Shattered into pieces. She took the flow of ecstasy, as waves of it crashed over her, leaving her weightless.

His kisses brought her back as he slid over her, pulling a condom on and settling his hips between her legs, his broad shoulders covering her. Protecting her. At that moment as she looked up into the eyes of the man above her, surrounding her with his body, feelings of pleasure and protection surrounding her, she felt safe.

"Please say yes, baby." His voice was strained as he kissed along her neck and jaw, his teeth scraping. She felt him at her entrance and realized that he was waiting for her permission. Emotion filled her. That he would ask her permission meant more to her than he would ever know.

She could tell that he was straining, tense with want, holding back from not just fucking her. His desire was at a crest of impatience, and she was high at the thought that she had that power over him.

"Yes," she whispered, trailing her hands up into his hair. She gasped and arched as he filled her in one slow, steady push till his hips were flush with hers and she was full with him.

Bringing one arm up above her head he leaned on his elbow, using it for balance. The other slid around her back, pulling her so she was arching up into him. He began to move. Slowly, deeply, and completely devastating every nerve ending she had.

She moaned as he started to move faster, flexing his powerful hips in toward her.

Filling her.

"God, baby." Wrecked, full of harsh pants, his hips stilled. She could hear him whispering curses to himself. His arms and chest shaking with the strain.

She ran her hands along his sweat-slicked back, loving the feel of his muscles twisting and twitching as he held himself back.

For her.

She loved it.

Slithering up his body, rubbing her chest against his with her mouth against his ear, she knew exactly what he needed. This wasn't about just her anymore. He had been patient. Trying even through the trouble they had gone through. It was her turn to give to him. And she would gladly do it a hundred times over.

"Let go," she whispered, licking the shell of his ear, and watched as the dam broke with that small act. He closed his eyes, his passion breaking across her as he thrust.

Hard.

Followed by another. And it built. More and more till she couldn't tell where he ended and she began.

Holding on and meeting him thrust for thrust, she started to build again. He was kissing her neck, nipping and biting his way across her jaw, driving her passion higher than she knew it could be. When he slid his arm out from under her and down till he was rubbing small slow circles over her clit in time with his thrusts, she knew that it was over for her. The beginning of another climax came at her like a freight train. With no end in sight.

"Get there, baby. Now," he grunted out, and she watched as he fought his own orgasm, determined to give her one more.

One last thrust was all it took, and she was flying over again, drifting away in ecstasy again. She listened as his breathing became choppy and heavy, then he lifted his head and, looking straight at her, he came.

She watched as it came over him and took it all. He dropped his head toward her chest as the last little tremor left their bodies. He rolled to the side and pulled her against him. She was floating on a cloud of air, content in the feelings that he gave her as she drifted to sleep.

Chapter 16

Dominic walked down the stairs of the old, abandoned warehouse to the basement that sat below. Not many people knew of this place, the stairs having been conveniently hidden. The warehouse itself sat back away from the road on the outskirts of town. Nobody came here. They were too scared of him. Or rather of what he represented. The Familia.

He didn't come here often. There wasn't often a time when his last name didn't make people bend to his control. Scared of the idea of what he could do, even if they were way off the mark. As much as people thought the Mafia was all about violence, it didn't often require as much as they thought. At least at his high ranking level.

He couldn't say that he would miss this part of his job. He had often dreaded walking down these steps, his training in this basement leaving a bad taste in his mouth. His father had tried to be the best father he could, but there were still parts of his childhood when he had to deal with the Boss of the Familia and not his dad. This basement was one of those places.

The blood.

The violence.

You could feel it in the air.

Because of her, for the first time in his life he looked forward to what was at the bottom of those stairs. He walked slowly, his shoes clicking against the concrete as he made his way down. He knew the men could hear him coming. Anticipation—he could taste it. He reached the bottom and casually took a glimpse around the room.

Rick was already there with a few of his other men, Danny having stayed at the house with Alice. Of the two men Danny was better at talking, putting people at ease. Rick was the opposite. He thrived on the violence.

As he glanced at the other men in the room he could feel the tension of excitement in the air at what was to come. It filled the air, surrounding the lone man who hung in the center of the room. His head was hanging in despair, arms strung up above him in chains that were wrapping, cutting into the skin, leaving a bloody crust against his skin. Infections had set into the swirl of bloody cuts covering his body. A work of art. His men had already started the fun. The message was clear.

Nobody touched what was his and got away with it.

Boris looked into his eyes, his face was filled with the fear of what was to come. Weak from the beatings he had already taken, his desperate moans filled the space. He didn't speak, though. He couldn't. His taped mouth ensured that Dominic wouldn't have to listen to the man's pitiful whining. It always grated on his nerves.

"Begin." Dominic's words rang out in the chilled room. Watching as his men began and the man's anguished cries rung in his ears.

For once he languished in the sound.

Hours later, in the early dawn, he slid into the front seat of his car. Driving home.

She was safe now. Protected.

As he drove his thoughts were consumed.

With her.

His Alice.

His never-ending obsession.

Three Months Later

She woke slowly, stretching her body as the twinge between her legs made her smile in remembrance. She looked over to the side of the bed and saw that Dominic was already gone. Although they both had their own rooms, he had started staying later with her at night and had on occasion fallen asleep after fucking her to sleep.

They had some ways to go in relearning each other after everything that had gone on, but it hadn't cooled their passion in the bedroom. If anything, it had helped to strengthen the bond between them. He seemed to almost be frantic with her, as if he didn't know if he could get enough. She was just as frantic to take everything that he could give her.

Outside of bed, he was gentle with her. Caring and almost loving. Doting on her and her needs. In the bedroom it was different. He took control. Using her body to the pleasure of them both. Dominic was such a contradiction. So passionate and forceful in one go. Gently holding her cheek to kiss her, and then holding her hands down and fucking her in an onslaught that left her barely able to think of anything but him.

He was hardly ever there in the mornings, leaving early so he could return throughout the day and spend it with her. So she wasn't surprised that he wasn't here this morning. It had been a wonderful month, though, and she couldn't have asked for more.

She was actually a little disappointed to be going back to school soon, and she knew that although he supported her wholeheartedly, he was disappointed to be sharing her time. He was almost greedy when it came to her, and she loved it. She remembered her parents together. Hardly a day apart without needing each other. When she was young she had hated it. Now she understood.

Things had been interesting at first after the incident with Geo. It had been hard on Dominic, knowing that he put her in that position. Once everything came out about Geo, his rules, and his actions toward her, Dom had lost it. It had taken her the better part of three days to get him settled down. He had vowed to hunt him down, but Geo had suspiciously disappeared. Which only enraged Dominic even further.

Even with Rick and Danny, she could tell that something was different. They were still the same with her, but they seemed more alert. And any time Geo was brought up their faces would become stone masks. She knew that all three of them felt guilty, Rick and Danny for letting it happen and blindly following what they thought were Dominic's orders. She didn't blame them at all and had tried telling them. She didn't think that anything short of Geo's head on a platter was going to make them happy.

Dominic was another matter. His anger and guilt over the whole thing sat heavily on him. After a few days of straightening out security protocols and sitting down with Rick and Danny, he decided it was okay for her to leave the house and the spoiling had begun. At least that was what he had called it. For her, though she liked spending time with him, it had been awful. She *did not* like shopping.

At first, she felt suffocated as he tried to overcompensate. Fancy dinners, jewelry. He had even taken the liberty of cleaning out the closet once he found out that she hadn't picked any of the clothes. Then he had taken her shopping.

She had thought that he would eventually settle down, but a week into it she had to have a talk with him.

"Dom, this isn't necessary," she had pleaded with him, his face melting just a little at the nickname that she had started calling him. The first time that she had accidentally called him that, he had gotten a weird look on his face. Later in bed, when she asked, he confided that he had never had a nickname from a woman. That they had never been around that long. Although she didn't want to hear about his past just like he *really* didn't want to hear about hers, she was relieved to know that what they had was special.

They had been standing in another jewelry store, a beautiful necklace and earring set with chocolate diamonds in a delicate setting placed in front of her. She was almost afraid to touch it.

"Do you not like it?" He had looked worried, and she didn't know what to do. Of course, she loved it, but this was the second set along with other miscellaneous pieces that he had bought in the last week. He needed to stop spending so much on her. It wasn't going to change her mind either way about staying with him, but she didn't think that he knew that exactly.

This has to stop, she had thought.

She had turned to him and, ignoring the man at the counter, placed her hands on his cheeks to get his attention. His gaze came to hers and she could see the troubling emotion there.

"Dom, I'm here because of you. Not all this," she had whispered, with a wave at the store in general.

"I don't need this. Just you." They had stared at each other, his look an odd mixture of hope and desperation that she knew all too well. She needed him to understand that she wasn't with him for the money or what he could give her. She was there for him. After a few seconds of hesitation, he turned to the salesclerk.

"Well take it," he said, and her mouth fell open at him blatantly disregarding what she had said.

"You like it, so you'll have it." As the salesclerk moved to box up the items, she had sighed in frustration. How could she make him see that this was too much!

"I need to set things right, sweetheart," he had told her, seeming to understand her frustration. "I brought you into my life with little regard for how it would affect you. Then I trusted you to someone else. Under me, you were harmed. Something that I vowed would never happen to you." He spoke quietly so that the clerk wouldn't overhear them.

"I promised to give you everything that you wanted and I didn't do that. So now I'll fix it and make this right. I know that you don't want my money. It's part of your appeal. But I want you to have everything you need and want." She had watched an emotion close to pain flash across his face and realized that this was still bothering him.

"Dominic, listen. None of this is your fault. And even if it was, buying me things wouldn't fix this. It's all on him, on Geo. It's okay that it all happened, though. I'm glad it did." He had looked horrified at her words, so she rushed to finish. "Look at how close we are now. I've never been this way with anybody else. I never let people in and now I'm with you. It's an amazing feeling. The whole thing, this mess, is okay because it gave me you. That's all I need."

His shoulders seemed to relax, taking her at her words, although she really doubted that he was going to drop the whole thing. She just needed him to stop spending this much. Honestly, she didn't even like shopping.

"Now will you please send that back! It's too much! I don't even know what I would wear it with." That wasn't completely true, since she had about fifty dresses now that would look great with it. The look he had sent her said he knew the same thing, and that nothing she said was going to dissuade him.

Then he had leaned forward and whispered in detail how she could pay him back that night. She had blushed bright red, which had sent him laughing. If red cheeks and a little embarrassment were the price to pay to hear him laugh, she would gladly pay it.

So things had been better, and at least there was less shopping. She knew that Dominic and his men were still searching for Geo, but she didn't ask. And he seemed happy to let her bury her head in the sand.

He had taken to rearranging his schedule so that he was home earlier in the afternoons, giving them the evening to spend together. She had also started to cook for him, too, and discovered that her man loved her cooking. She had never done it much because she had lived by herself and groceries were scarce but, being in his kitchen with unlimited supplies, she was having a blast trying new recipes.

When Christmas came they enjoyed a small affair. Neither of them had any sort of holidays the last few years, so she was happy with the intimate way things had turned out.

They set up a small tree and decorated it in between stealing kisses from each other. There had been way too many gifts for her under the tree. She would never tell him, but she secretly enjoyed it. She had gotten him a simple picture frame with her picture in it for his desk. She hadn't known what to get him, and she wanted to use her money to buy it, so she was limited on what she could get him. But based on his reaction, he had loved it.

So much in fact that he ended up showing her how much right there under the Christmas tree. It would be a moment that she would never forget.

He seemed to not be able to get enough of her, and honestly the man was more than anything she had even hoped for in bed. She couldn't get enough, either. She wasn't a virgin before they had met, but she wasn't experienced either. He was showing her a side of sex that she never knew existed. No wonder people always acted like it was the best thing since sliced bread.

She had started to trust him more, too. Telling him more about her life before him. Trying to let him in with small little tidbits about her life and her parents, and he seemed to soak them up. He never pushed for more than she was willing to give him, though.

She knew that he was waiting for her to tell him about her time with her uncle, and had hinted a couple of times that he would be there when she was. It was interesting that he knew so much about him already, but she wasn't going to bring it up just yet.

It wasn't that she didn't trust him. She was starting to realize that if she could trust anyone, it would be him. It was just that she didn't want to talk about it. She knew that he would be angry, and things had been going so well that she didn't want to jinx it. She was finally happy.

She felt like herself, from before her parents had passed. The dark cloud that hung over her head was now gone, replaced with something that was more than she had ever hoped for. Living with him, sharing their life together, and having someone that she knew cared for her and would keep her safe. It wasn't just happiness, it was love.

But how did she tell him that?

Chapter 18

She rolled over and looked at the clock, seeing that it was almost nine. She decided to get up and shower and get ready. She was supposed to go to the campus today to get her new books. She was still going to get used ones, even though Dominic wouldn't like it. He would just have to get used to it. There was no reason to spend that much money on schoolbooks.

She walked into her closet, all clean from her shower, and looked for something to wear. It now held jeans and shirts, still designer but definitely more her style. Of course, there was still a section of fancy wear toward the back, but it was all things that she and Dominic had picked out together. After getting dressed, she made her way downstairs.

The smell of coffee was in the air and she walked a little faster in anticipation, thinking that Dominic must have started some before he left. When she turned the corner into the kitchen she saw him. Hair mussed and wearing nothing but pajama pants low on his hips leaning against the kitchen bar reading the newspaper, a cup of coffee next to him. A thrill went through her full of desire. She really was a lucky woman.

"Dom."

He looked up from his paper with a roguish grin, as if he knew the effect he had on her. It was okay, though; she knew that she had the same effect on him, too.

"Baby, you didn't think I'd let you go get school all settled without me, did you?" he said teasingly.

She smiled and rushed toward him. Although he had made time for her, he hadn't been able to take an actual day off in a couple of weeks and she missed the one-on-one time with him. She reached him and the force of her body against his pushed him flush against the counter. Her hands went around his neck at the same time that his slid around her waist. The kiss he gave her was heated and full of promise. One that she knew he would fulfill.

As quickly as the kiss started he flipped their positions and had her against the fridge, taking control of their kiss and deepening it. Her hands slid into his hair to bring him closer. Passion so thick between them like it always was made her breath stall. His hand cupped her breast and fingers twisted her nipple with just the right amount of pain that she knew he loved to give. She was happy to take it.

Their kisses left her breathless as his movements seemed to grow in aggression, and she knew that he was losing control. Frantically they clawed at each other's clothes as they nipped and kissed with a frenzied passion that was rising by the second. He shoved her pants down and slid his hands between her folds, slick with desire for him, as her head fell back on her shoulders, unable to hold it up as he brought her right up to her peak. Cupping her neck to hold her in place, he whispered,

"Come." A single command.

It was his voice.

His movements.

It was just him.

She was so far gone that she crashed, wave after wave of sweet passion coursing through her.

Moments later, his harsh breathing in her ear, he was still slowly twisting his fingers inside her, keeping her passion high. She twisted her hand between them to grasp him. Hard and weeping, she knew that she didn't have much time to play.

He was always frantic in his desire toward her. As if he couldn't get enough. That it would never be enough. And she knew just how he felt because she felt the same.

Only a few twists of her hand on his shaft and he was shoving her to the floor, her knees crashing on the tile as he grabbed her neck and forced her down—her ass up high, waiting for him. With one hand holding her down, the other guided himself into her.

With one thrust he slid in deep.

Hard.

Delicious.

She would never get enough of this, of him.

He paused and she looked over her shoulder to see his head thrown back, jaw clenched.

"Christ!" His exclamation was followed by a thrust, then another. Till he was grasping her hips and fucking her with all the that he had. All she could do was hold on and enjoy all that he was giving her.

This was trust. Her in submission to his desire. Him letting her see the side of him that no one ever saw. Wild, uncontrolled, unbridled passion. It was one of the greatest gifts that he would ever give her.

"Fuck yes, that's it," was his response as she clenched around him, sailing over again for the second time. Smaller than the first, but no less consuming. One. Two. Three thrusts later and he stilled inside her. Filling her with everything he had. His hands softened as their passion cooled, and they both sank to the floor in each other's arms.

***

"Do I have you all day?" she asked, starting to make plans in her head. They lay there panting on the floor. The tile was cold on her back, but it didn't bother her. She was happy to be anywhere with him.

"Good God, baby. Give a man a little time to rest." His grin said it all and she lightly tapped his shoulder in rebuke.

"You're the one that couldn't seem to keep it in your pants. I was just on my way to get some coffee and, boom, here I am on the floor." She was giggling as she said it, but at the mention of the floor he swooped her up and carried her toward her room.

"You really need another round?" she asked, shocked. He had great stamina, but even he needed a little bit of a break! Which was fine with her; she was normally so wrung out by the time they had both come, that she needed the break, too.

"No smartass, I'm taking us to shower. If I get carried away in there, well then, who's to stop me." She giggled.

He didn't stop at her room though, just kept going. To the wide double doors at the end of the hall, where she knew his room was. She had been in there on occasion but until now they had maintained separate rooms. Although he did sleep in her room at night.

She had asked him once why, and he had said that he didn't want to push her. That he couldn't stand not being with her, but that didn't mean that he had to bulldoze her. She had smiled at his brand of chivalry. So pushy and sweet all in the same moment.

He carried her to the bathroom and set her down, making sure she was steady before letting go. She threw her hair up into a high bun to keep it from getting wet and watched him. Turning the water on full blast, he drew her in with him.

She stood with her back to the water, letting it run over her as she stared at Dominic in front of her. She had just had a shower, but she didn't really want to spend the day wandering all over with him leaking down her thighs.

He grabbed his body wash and dumped a bunch in his hands. Then starting at her shoulders, he washed her, working clear down to her feet. He stood back up and slid his hand gently between her legs, rubbing, making her part her legs and moan as desire started to flame again. Stepping back, he chuckled at her frown.

"No more, or we will never leave." She had to shake her head to realize why exactly that wasn't a good idea.

She was still in awe that this man was here with her. She knew that there was real love out there. After all, her parents had had it, and she knew that she was falling harder in love each day with this complicated man. She just hoped that he felt the same.

He finished and turned her body into the water to rinse off. Standing behind her with his hands wrapped around her, he rested his chin on her shoulder. They stood silent for a while, soaking up each other's company as the water poured over them.

"I want you to move in with me," he whispered. She paused at his words.

Wasn't she already living with him? Sure they had separate bedrooms, but he had taken care of her lease and she hadn't been back to her old apartment.

He must have sensed her quietness and mistook it because he continued, "I want you in my bed, baby, no more separate spaces. With me every morning when I wake up. I want to fall asleep with you every night. I know it's only been a couple of months, but I'm not the type of man that is going to let you have your own space and only see you on dates once or twice a week. I've been giving you as much space as I can, but you're mine, and I can't take it anymore. I want you here, in my arms every night."

She turned around and wrapped her arms around his neck, studying his face. He seemed nervous, which was a contradiction to the man she was used to, and she didn't like it. He was always so sure of himself and confident. She didn't like that he was worried about her answer, so she gave him what he wanted.

"Yes," was all she said, but it was enough.

His shoulders dropped, a smile coming over his face as he visibly relaxed. As his lips found hers and he backed her up against the shower wall, she had one thought.

This was exactly where she wanted to be.

Chapter 19

Taking a deep breath, she double-checked her list in her hands. She was done; well, almost, but everything else could wait. She just needed notebooks, then that was it. Looking around, she spotted Dom leaning against the wall by the front door. She knew that he was bored, but she still appreciated him coming.

Any time she looked toward him, she found his eyes on her. Tracking her across the room to each place that she needed to be. Not being pushy and in her space, giving her what she needed but still being there. Protecting her. Protecting what was his.

Still, between getting her class schedule and standing in line for her books, she hadn't been able to talk to him much. She gave him a small smile and he grinned back at her.

She stepped up to pay when it was her turn. Gathering everything and taking her receipt, she walked up to him. He took her bags and wrapped an arm around her back, leading her out of the building.

"That all you need, sweetheart?" He leaned down to ask in her ear. She simply nodded because there was no way she was going to be able to talk. He left her tongue-tied more often than she liked to admit, and he grinned. He knew exactly what he did to her.

"Lunch?" His words a more a statement than a question and he started leading her toward the car. She had been surprised when they left that morning with nobody coming with them. He never left the house without some sort of security with him—her either, for that matter.

Geo leaving after the whole debacle had set him on edge. She figured that he was assuming like her that both Geo and Melissa had left town and were never coming back. They would be stupid to ever show their faces again.

He drove them to a little café downtown, where they were seated at a window seat toward the back of the restaurant.

After the waiter took their orders, getting a hard glare from Dom because he continued staring at her, she settled back and relaxed, looking out over the snowy ground. She loved winter, but she would be glad when spring was here.

"How many classes do you have left?" he questioned.

"Two." She was nearly hopping in her seat in excitement, and he grinned at her as if she actually had. "I'm so excited to almost be done."

"We haven't ever talked about what you want to do when you get done." He studied her, his dark stare taking in far too much.

"I don't know. The plan was to just get a job. Any job really." He nodded in thought and then looked to her again.

"If you could do anything you wanted, money and school notwithstanding, what would it be?" His question stumped her. What would she do? The plan was to always just be able to support herself and not need anyone. But these last few weeks of not working and simply enjoying her time with Dominic had been some of the best of her life.

She remembered long ago, before her parents died, she loved to paint and draw and had always wanted to go out and be able to help people in her community. But then come home to a family of her own. She had always felt lonely as an only child and knew that she wanted more when her time came.

But she didn't know what she wanted now. Did she still want the same things? She didn't have the high aspirations that she knew most women had. Would that drive him away? She worried that it was too domesticated, even for him. He lived in the city, worked in the city. He lived in a modern penthouse. Everything that was the opposite of that long-ago dream. She really was stumped. She looked at him and he gave her a small, sad smile.

Leaning forward, he wrapped her hands in his.

"I used to paint," she told him, letting him in just a little more.

"Really?" He seemed so surprised that she giggled.

"I haven't in a long time, but yeah." He squeezed her hands and she looked back to him.

"Baby, you've spent so long just trying to survive." He paused as if not knowing how to continue. "Is that what you would like to do?" He looked so concerned at that moment that she felt a little of her heart melt. He was always looking out for her.

She shrugged because she didn't know. It seemed like a lifetime ago. Almost as if that girl was long gone.

"Think about it, okay?" She nodded.

119

The rest of the meal went smoothly, but his words rang in her head. And by the end of the meal she was so lost in thought that when he stood to take a call he had to shake her shoulder to get her attention.

"I have to take this," he said with a worried look on his face. She put a smile on and nodded to him. As he walked away she could see his demeanor change.

It was one of the things that she was getting used to. It was like he was two different people. The man he was with her, then the man who ran his night clubs with an iron fist. He was demanding and ruthless. It was a contradiction to the sweet, concerned man whispering in her ear. She figured that his business probably needed him like that. She didn't know a lot about what exactly he did. She just knew that he ran several clubs across the U.S., that he had some sort of merger with his businesses going on right now, and that he somehow had ties to the Mafia. Or his family did. She wasn't really sure.

Although she had heard rumors about the Mancini Family, he had never mentioned anything about it or his family. It wasn't a talk that had come up, but she wasn't blind. The calls, the demeanor changes, the security. There was something else there. He had given her space, though, so she figured the least she could do was to give him the same. She trusted him to tell her eventually. Just like she knew she would tell him about her past.

She glanced out the window, taking the last sips of her drink, mulling over her choices of whether to talk to Dominic or not, about his family and their different views of dreams of the future. Could she stay with him if he didn't see the same future that she did?

She didn't even know if that was still a dream for her. Did she want the whole marriage and family thing? The pang in her chest gave her the answer she was looking for. Yes, she did. She wanted what her parents had. However, the thought of talking about it with Dom was scary enough for her to keep it to herself a little longer.

Deep in thought, she glanced out the window and down the street to a man who was leaning against a street post. It caught her as odd because it wasn't a bus stop and the people around him were walking, moving around him, headed to their destinations. He had on sunglasses and a dark leather jacket, making him stand out even more in the artistic hub of downtown. Slowly, her gaze glued to him, he raised his hand and tipped his glasses up then let them fall back in place just as slowly.

The eyes.

She would never forget eyes like that. Scalding with hatred.

Geo!

Fear shot up her spine. She jerked her head around quickly, looking for Dominic, but she couldn't see him. Her gaze flew back to the man, to see him smirk as if he could sense her fear.

A finger salute then he was turning and blending in with the crowd, walking away. She sat there frozen in place, stunned. Did Dominic know he was here? And why did it feel like she was being left in the dark? What didn't she know? And that evil smirk when he saluted her. It was sending chills all over her body. Somehow it felt as if there was nothing that was okay about any of this.

She gathered her purse and stood, her only thought to get to Dominic. She stumbled through the restaurant, weaving through the tables until she finally spotted him on the phone by the front door. She jetted across the restaurant, fear clawing her insides making her feel as if she was going to throw up. She knew that some of the fear was irrational, but somehow she knew that something was very wrong and she had to get to Dominic

"Dominic!" she cried out before she launched herself toward him. His arm came up to wrap around her.

"What the fuck," he grumbled. Then, catching the look on her face and the tremble in her body, his face lost all confusion, and he became alert immediately.

"Tell me," he ordered. She was so shocked by seeing Geo that she didn't register the change in his tone.

"Geo … He was there … on the street … Did you …" She wanted to ask if he knew that Geo had been here but she couldn't get it out.

"Shit." He looked around and started toward the door, pulling her with him and dialing on his phone at the same time.

"Call Bruno," he said to whoever was on the phone. "She said she saw him. *NOW*! Find me that fucker." He shut the phone off and shoved her out the door and to the car. And before she knew it they were down the street, racing away.

"Where was he?" he demanded, his head flinging back and forth, checking all the mirrors.

She told him everything that she had seen, hanging on to the car handle for dear life. Dominic was weaving in and out between cars, not stopping for anything, not even the lights. Her fear that Geo was still a threat obviously holding some truth, as he raced them toward the penthouse and away from the bistro.

"Dom … Did you know he was going to be there?" His stony 'fuck no' was her answer.

"Can you tell me what's going on?" she pleaded quietly. She had a feeling deep in her gut that something more was going on. It wasn't making sense to her. Why would Geo come back? He had to know that Dom was looking for him. And if that was true, why was Dominic holding back from her?

He turned to look at her, his face set hard. She kept his stare, hoping for anything long after he looked away. In the past month he had opened up, and she had gotten good at reading him. Now, though, his face was a blank mask. Nothing. No emotion. A chill went down her spine at the realization that there was more going on.

Something that wasn't good.

It didn't matter anymore to her what it was. She knew without a doubt that she would take it and shoulder it, no matter how heavy. He might not know where she stood, but she did. She loved him. Words weren't needed. She would show him. She knew what she wanted.

A home. A family. Something to call her own. Nothing else mattered except them. It was funny how a small sprint through a restaurant could change your view of life. All she had been thinking about was finding him. Now it was her turn to shoulder some of his burden.

She watched as he seemed to come to some conclusion and, shaking his head, he sighed. He pulled into the parking garage and parked. The silence echoed after their speedy run through the city. She glanced at him. His hands clenched the wheel and his jaw ticked in anger. She could feel it radiating off him.

"There are things about me that you don't know." His voice was jerky and angry, as if he was upset for having to speak at all.

She wondered if maybe she had been right, and pushing him to talk was not the right thing. But she needed to know since this concerned her, too.

She gently placed her hand on his arm and he looked at her and then at her hand. Sighing, he leaned back in his seat and started to open his door.

"This is not a conversation for the car."

Chapter 20

He led her upstairs, his arm wrapped around her tight. This time entering the apartment, they didn't stop; he led her straight to his office. She had only been in here several times, but this time, entering the big double doors at the end of the hall, nerves suddenly seized her.

He led them to a couch on the far wall set up with a couple of chairs in a simple seating arrangement. He unbuttoned his suit jacket and leaned back into the corner of the couch, making a clear statement of trying to stay far away from her. She watched him as he gazed around the room, till he came to her. His gaze still dark and cold.

"My family has a long history here in the Midwest. Chicago was once one of the most feared cities for its crime. Over time though those families spread out, looking for new territory, and my family settled here. That of course was a few generations ago. Back then they were the typical family or my version of a typical family. You would have called them Mafia." He paused and looked down at her face, as if to gauge what she was thinking. She had already figured out that he came from something along those lines, with Taby's talk, but she just didn't know how he fit into it.

"You knew?" he questioned, running his fingers through his hair in agitation, showing a small glimpse of emotion before he shut it down again. She was starting to feel cold. Sitting on the other side of the couch from him, she felt lightyears away from the man she had come to love.

"No, but I suspected something was up; your family's name is pretty well known. Also, Taby had all kinds of stories." She smiled at him, trying to lighten the mood, but he didn't react. Just nodded and continued.

"Well I won't go into detail, but if you ever watched a movie about gangsters or read a book I'm sure you're imagining things—most of them true back then."

"Did they sell stuff ... like illegally?" she whispered, horrified at where this might be going. Not being able to think about him selling women and everything that went with that. He nodded.

"Guns, drugs, booze, even women. They did it all. But times changed and so did our family. My grandfather didn't want the family to follow him in that legacy, but you don't just leave the Familia. You are not just a part of it, it runs in our blood. Blood in, blood out."

"So he took us in another direction. Gambling has always been a very lucrative avenue, but my grandfather took it to another level, and my father continued in his footsteps. This continued till I was sixteen, when my grandfather died."

She braved a chance and reached out to him, laying her hand on his arm. She knew how it felt to lose a relative, someone close to you. He lay his hand over hers briefly, then moved slightly and her hand dropped. She pulled it back and watched him as he continued to stare out the window across the room.

"He had always wanted his children out of the business, and to be able to choose their way. Their own passion. When I was young he used to always tell me that when I grew up I could be anything I wanted to be." He sighed big, as if the memory was painful.

"Anyway, he never made it possible. A year after he passed my mother was killed and my father took her death hard. He then took it upon himself to finish my grandfather's dream. To get the family out. So he started working with other families. Most didn't like it, but one family, the Russians, wanted to help. Slowly they bought out our territory as we settled all debts."

She thought back to that night in the restaurant, about Danny's toast to Dom.

> *"Here's to Dom! To following his grandfather's wish and getting us all out of the Family!"*

Now it all made sense.

"You finished it."

"Yes. Well, my father finished it. I was only a part of giving away the last of our local assets. As of now, I am not Familia."

"The night clubs?"

"Those are mine. I needed something to live off and, honestly, I couldn't see myself doing anything other than business, I'm good at it and I like it. So off my father's gambling contacts, I started my night club, all legit. Now it's turned into five."

He said it like it was something that wasn't a big deal, when she knew it was the exact opposite. A shot of pride shot through her at what he had done and accomplished in such a short amount of time. Then a thought occurred to her.

127

"So why all the men, then? You always have bodyguards and men around. Surely running a night club isn't that dangerous?" she questioned.

"You're right. However, I still have my family name. When I opened my first club, my father gifted me five men. They have been with me ever since."

"Geo." His already blank face seemed to grow even colder at the mention of the man's name.

"Yes, he was one of them who was gifted to me. I once thought that he was a friend. He helped me run my business. He was trusted." This last part was said bitterly, and she felt sad that she might have been the one to bring this on him.

"Geo is a complication. See, I don't run every club. I oversee the men who run them. Geo was what was essentially my right-hand man. He was trusted. That trust was earned until things didn't seem to be adding up. Slowly I had men reporting small dips in the cash. Nothing big. But we couldn't find where it was coming from even when I brought it up to the employees; nobody knew anything. Then things with you started happening. Geo was supposed to be watching you when you were working at the restaurant, but he never reported any incidents."

His jaw clenched and then reached out for her hand, turning it over to study the faint scars from the burns she had suffered.

"Then the whole debacle with Melissa and his treatment of you. But before we could bring him in, he disappeared."

"Is the money still disappearing?" she asked, wondering if Geo was the one taking it.

"Yes." His answer was short. He dropped her hand and leaned back into the couch again, his gaze, cold and chilling, directed straight at her. Studying her.

"So maybe he had a partner?" At his chilling smile to her question, she felt her eyes widen. Fear slithered along her every nerve.

"That's exactly what we think, baby." His use of 'baby' was condescending. "I just can't find him. We thought that he had disappeared. It's been weeks and there has been no sign of him. The fucker's gone to ground. We had just assumed that the two incidents were separate." He ground out the last bit. She tried not to let his voice get to her. She knew that he was upset about the whole situation. There was still one thing that was bothering her about this whole situation, not that any of it was all that good.

"If you knew that Geo was stealing, why did you put him with me? Why didn't you ask him earlier?" He sighed, deep and weary, and she saw a flash of guilt go through his eyes before it was gone.

"Because I trusted him. It's hard to hear something that you don't want to hear. I didn't want to think it was him. None of us did." She thought about it and realized that it was true. She wouldn't believe something or someone if they had been telling her that Taby was stealing from her.

"None of this should ever have come back to you. But I can't hide you from it anymore. You need to be aware that Geo is out there and I don't know what he will do. I won't let him touch you." His statement was firm and his eyes were solemn, finally showing the emotion underneath, conveying that he would do anything to make sure she was safe.

"There are two of you," she blurted out, then blushed as she realized she had voiced her thoughts out loud. His puzzled look said he had no idea what she was talking about.

"There is this hard man who controls his world with a firm hand. Who your men defer to and people are afraid of." She stopped and studied his face.

"Then there is my Dom. The man I feel safe with, the man who holds me and makes love to me, and whispers 'baby' in my ear." She moved across the couch till she was pressed against him, and she gently reached up and cupped his cheek.

"Does it confuse you?" he whispered. Their faces were so close that their breath was mingling.

"No. I know who you are. No matter who I get. I know I'm safe, and …" She paused, unsure if she should voice her feelings so soon.

"And?" he prodded. She could see the emotion in his eyes of what she was about to say. She could see that he wanted it. He wanted those words.

"And with the man I love."

With her words, his lips crushed hers.

Chapter 21

The elevator doors swooshed open and Alice walked into the penthouse. She was exhausted. The day had been filled with helping Taby shop for furniture for their new house. She was happy for her friend that they were finally getting on the right track and were able to move forward with their life. For months now they had been living in crappy housing and barely making ends meet. Now that Troy had finally found a good job, he was able to provide them with the life they needed.

It had been two weeks since the day she had gone and gotten her books and they had talked in his office. Normally her time would be filled with classes and homework, but this being her last semester, it was really light. She only had two classes, and she was lucky that Taby had one of them, too.

Because Taby hadn't had a trust fund to help her through all the bills for school, she was farther behind than Alice. She would always be grateful for what her parents had given her.

Since her time was open more she found herself almost bored for the first time in her life. She had baked enough to feed an army, and Rick and Danny were loving it. Complaining that they were going to get fat with her around. But one can only bake so much, and she was still bored.

So she took off down the hall to see if Dom was in his office. She didn't really want to bother him, but she needed something to do other than just sit around. She knocked on the door and heard him tell her to come in. Walking in, however, she was unsure when she saw that there were a few other men in there with him.

"Sorry, I can come back," she said as she turned to make her way back out the door.

"No. We're done." She could tell that she had interrupted something important. His jaw was ticking and his mood seemed to fill the room with anger. She quietly stepped out of the doorway for the men to leave, Danny and Rick with them, but not even one of them looked in her direction.

"Is everything okay?" she asked.

He just nodded, and she became nervous when he wouldn't look at her. The last few weeks had been great, but he had become increasingly busy and they hadn't had a chance to talk much.

Maybe he was upset that she still hadn't shared everything about her past. He wasn't pushing her, but time was running out. He deserved to know the truth. He walked over to the couch and beckoned her over to him. She walked to where he was and stood in front of him, not wanting to take up too much of his time. She realized now that she shouldn't have come in here; he was always busy during the day and his job was important to him. She needed to get used to that. He reached forward and grabbed her around her hips and placed her on his lap.

"How are you?" he asked as he leaned forward and settled her better on his lap. She could tell that something was still wrong, his body was tense, but she didn't want to pry.

"I'm good," she said instead of telling him the real reason that she was down here. He didn't need to hear her whine about herself.

"Hmmm." His hands slipped under her shirt and his fingers ran along her bra edge, teasing her with his touch. She could feel him harden under her, and although she knew something was going on she let it go and focused on the feeling of being with him.

Whatever was going on, it hadn't affected the way that he still wanted her. She tilted her head back to give him more room as he started kissing along her collarbone. She moaned as one hand slipped around and squeezed her tighter to him, and his hips slightly bucked and he rubbed himself up against her. Her breath was now catching deep in her chest as she reached for his shirt, when a knock on the door startled her.

Jumping up, she tried to scramble off his lap. He stood and wrapped his arm around her as the door opened, giving her a slight kiss on the neck.

"Stay," was all he whispered. Then he walked them to the meeting table and chairs across the room and sat down, pulling her down to sit curled into him. Only then did she turn her attention toward the person who had walked in. She was curious to see that it was a woman and she was standing just inside the door, her mouth open and staring at them.

"What?" Dom barked, and the woman visibly jerked. Pulling herself together she walked in toward them, carrying several folders stacked up high.

"You have four minutes," he said in a cold voice, and she frowned in confusion. While he always seemed harsh in this environment, he seemed to be extra short with this woman.

She thought back to when she came in and realized that he hadn't relaxed at all that much even after they had started to make out. She laid her hand on his chest to reassure and calm him. She knew that he noticed but he didn't acknowledge her. He only seemed to be getting more upset as the woman continued to stare at them.

"Now, Brittany!" he barked, and even Alice jumped. Quickly, the woman— whose name was apparently Brittany— started rambling.

"Sir, I have the papers for what you asked for. The quarterly reports are the same as last week. A fifth lower than the expected income. However, the visitation reports all show a fifteen percent increase." The woman was visibly shaking and Alice wondered why she seemed so nervous. Her gaze kept sweeping between Dominic and the man on the door. Alice had never seen him before, and guessed that he was from the club's security team.

"That's enough. Go." His words were just as clipped as before. Brittany practically threw the stack of folders at them before rushing out the door.

"What was that?" she asked, bewildered, but he simply gestured for her to wait.

"Go." He spoke to the man at the door. "Follow her and report. Remember what I said."

"Yes, sir." And with that, it was just the two of them again.

"I want you to look at something." That really wasn't what she thought he was going to say. Of course, she would help in any way that she could. She just didn't know how. He walked over to the stack of folders and placing them on the table, pulled out a chair for her. He seemed to think about his words then nodded to her.

"Tell me what you see."

She sat down, looking at everything in front of her. It was weekly and quarterly reports from one of his nightclubs. A relatively new one located in Florida. She knew that he thought that it was going to be a moneymaker from their previous talks. She looked at him again, but he was simply staring at her. Emotionless. Again. She shivered remembering the last time that he had acted like that. It wasn't good. But she did what he asked and started to read the reports.

The more she got into the report, though, she could see that it was losing money hand over fist. The gaps in the losses didn't make any sense to her, and she couldn't find the connections between the losses and the account that they were connected to.

"Who does these reports?" she asked, continuing to read.

"Brittany does." He sighed and sat down across from her. Running his hands through his hair, he looked exhausted and worried.

"Are you okay?" She knew that this was weighing on him. Then add the mess with Geo and she knew that he had a lot on his plate.

"Brittany was one of Melissa's friends." Her back went ramrod straight at the mention of that woman. "And with everything going on, her association with them puts her in a bad place."

135

"Okay."

"Normally she would report to Geo and he would cover the financial assets. He has a man who does the paperwork for him that we're not using anymore." His tone was harsh and she could see he was trying to hold himself back. She was starting to think that something more was going on again. She didn't know why that caused a pain in her heart. Every time something went wrong they ended up having to jump some hurdle. Was this going to be like that?.

"Do think you might have found his accomplice?" she asked studying him.

"Interesting that you would say that," he said, throwing her for another loop.

She could practically see the steam coming out of his ears as he jerked his phone out of his pocket and dialed a number.

"I need Geo's files here now … yes." Then he clicked off. He turned and stared at her, his jaw ticking. She sat still, not knowing what he needed or what she should do.

The door opened and in walked Danny and Rick with another man, all carrying boxes. They sat them on the table along the far wall and walked out, and she started to feel a prickle of unease go through her.

"Dom …" she started to ask, but he ignored her and stood up, walking over to the boxes and flipping one open.

"The way that the family ventures are set up is that each man reports to a higher man till you reach the Capo or Boss. Geo had been traded through a couple of different families before he was gifted to me." He was searching through the files as he talked.

"Traded?" she questioned in confusion.

"Often, men are not suited to their position, or in some cases there is a need for a fresh face that hasn't been recognized yet. In this case, some of the families trade men. Geo was one of them. He worked his way up to being my lieutenant within two years, which was almost unheard of. He was trusted by my men and me. But we never really stopped to think about where his origin was from. Families have in the past sent spies into other organizations to gain information." He paused and gave her a look that she couldn't decipher. Then looked back to his box and continued.

"As such, new recruits are subject to ..." He paused and shook his head. "Well, we make sure they are going to be loyal, put it that way." His smirk with his words had a cruel twist to it, one that she hadn't seen from him before. This was the man who ran the Familia.

I'm glad that I'm not on his bad side, she thought.

"Anyway, there's a family on the West Coast, they run the West Coast Crime Syndicate. They have often butted heads with my father and grandfather and their methods leading our Familia away from a more traditional route. It makes it harder to complete a line from west to east."

She had so many questions rolling through her head but she didn't say anything, letting him continue with his story. Although his family terrified her, she was interested to know his history.

"When Geo started recruiting people under him to do the menial tasks such as accounting," he said with a pointed look to the paperwork spread out before her, "we started to notice that a lot of West Coast connections were happening. Anything from supplies to contractors, the majority of them were clearly from out west. Slowly all my clubs started to use them. Which puzzled us because, being so widespread, you would go to the closest vendor for that specific club."

"That makes sense." Then another piece of what he had said clicked into place.

"Geo is a spy?"

"Was. Yes, and we suspect his sister Melissa. Which puts every person that he has brought on a liability. Eventually we will find him and get our answers."

She nodded, knowing that his version of questioning probably wouldn't be very nice. He might not be Familia anymore, but right now he was certainly acting like he was. She shivered at the thought.

"How would this affect you now, though? You aren't a part …" She trailed off, not wanting to label his family in front of him.

"Even though my clubs are not run by Familia, my family's name is still well known. Geo was one of the men gifted to me, and I suspected that he wasn't happy with his placement or with me leaving, but nothing was ever said. Then after the money started disappearing, we couldn't make any connections."

"There is only one problem." His tone was still off as he walked stiffly to his desk and drew a folder from one of the drawers. She had thought that the way he was acting was due to the situation or the day, but now she wasn't so sure.

His face was a blank mask, his body stiff, and he was never like that with her. His gaze gave her a chill that went straight to her bones. She glanced around and saw that they weren't alone anymore either. There were three men in the room, all blocking the doors, and she suddenly feared that what he was about to say wasn't good at all.

"Dom?" she questioned, but he didn't answer her. Instead he walked up to where she was sitting and tossed a folder down in front of her. She stared at it, not sure what he wanted her to do.

"This man is from one of the West Coast Crime Syndicates. The main lieutenant. He, as of earlier this month, is now the Capo, the leader. He was Geo's boss. And he is a man that we cannot find, cannot track. We know nothing about him. He is just a black hole. We only have his name and a simple picture." He stared down at her coolly.

"We?" she asked

"My Familia." His voice was hard.

"You're working for the Familia again?" she asked fearfully. His past had always scared her, and he had promised that he wasn't or wouldn't in the future ever be a part of it.

"No. But when someone threatens my house, my men, it will be dealt with." His answer was short and her heart hurt at his words, at the way he was acting. But he didn't answer her, instead commanding her.

"Open it." He nodded to the folder in front of her. She stared back at him, hoping to see anything that would resemble that man she loved. But that man was locked up tight and here in front of her was not her Dominic, but the son of the Familia. And he wasn't to be messed with.

She slowly leaned forward and opened the folder, peeling back the front page. There was a picture of a man with red hair, a long nose, and full cheeks. He was smiling at a point away from the camera, but even his smile invoked a chill up her spine. There was a faint scar cut horizontally over his cheek. It was a scar that she knew well. She had given it to him.

139

The picture in front of her was none other than her uncle.

"Say Geo was to recruit a pretty little brown-haired girl. One that was part of his organization. One that he knew I would fall for. One that would be perfectly placed to get the information they need." The words, cold and brutal, slapped against her skin. What was he asking her?

She felt her breathing growing faint. Her head started to spin and fear started to clutch her chest. Her hands were shaking as she pressed them to her chest, trying to rub the sudden ache of fear away. The edges of her vision were swimming as she stared at his blurring face.

Still carrying that hard look, his eyes showed no emotion toward her. She watched as his jaw ticked. Her thoughts swirled in her head right up till the darkness swallowed her.

It wasn't just Geo who they thought was a spy.

He thought she was one.

Chapter 22

Dominic sat in a chair in the corner of the room, his thoughts in turmoil. He couldn't bring himself to wake her. The look on her face as she stared at him before she passed out would forever haunt him.

He knew that she had a past. He knew that there were demons in her past, he had seen them before in her eyes, but he didn't push. He had thought that they would have longer. He hadn't wanted to ruin what was happening between them any more than she had.

But once again he had fucked it all up. He had let his emotions get the best of him, and treated her like gutter trash. *Again.* He couldn't seem to stop fucking up around her. He should have just sat her down and talked to her. She always had such an open face, it was easy to read her. He would have gotten his answers, whether they were the ones he liked or not.

What if everyone was right, what if she was a spy? They knew that she was connected to the new West Coast Capo, they just didn't know how. It was a huge coincidence that she was here now with all the fucking crap up in the air with Geo.

He took a deep breath and leaned his head back into his chair, moments of them flashing through his mind. Them eating breakfast, her moaning his name, writhing in his bed, her hair spread around her.

The moment that she said that she loved him.

He felt another tug as he remembered the exact moment that he had fallen in love with her. He had never told her, hadn't returned it when she had told him. Too ecstatic with her declaration and fucking her right then and there on his office couch.

He saw that moment every time he looked at that couch now. He wasn't sure if he was sad or happy that he hadn't told her that he loved her, too. He thought that they would have time. Now, he didn't know what they had. A slight tap at the door broke his thoughts and he got up to answer it. He cracked it open to find Danny with Rick standing in the hall, their faces drawn and tight. He knew that they had grown to care for her as well, and that they didn't like the way things were looking any more than he did.

He stepped through the door and closed it softly behind him, not wanting to wake her just yet. They all stood there, none of them wanting to actually broach the subject that was just behind the door. He didn't know what he would do if it turned out to be true.

She had become his whole world. He couldn't picture his life without her. But if she was a spy? How would they continue?

"Do you think she actually did it?" The voice was slight and pained and sounded nothing like the Danny that he knew. They had practically grown up together. And he had always been the joker. That he was this solemn and withdrawn spoke to his depth of feeling toward Alice.

Not knowing how to answer, he just dropped his head. He hoped with everything in him that she wasn't there for some nefarious reason. But he needed to talk to her. He couldn't be the idiot that just accepted her words. People were counting on him.

This whole thing had brought him to realize that, although he knew her basic story and he was starting to share a life with her, he still didn't know her. He didn't know her past and how that had shaped her to be who she was. Other than simple things, he hardly knew anything about the girl he had come to love.

He knew other things, though. How she was a fierce friend, how loyal she was. She was kind and giving, and she hated spending his money. He chuckled internally at that thought and the memories of them shopping.

She liked ketchup on her turkey sandwich, and she could bake a cake to make a man weep over. She was deep and her feelings ran strong, both things that he knew extended to him and the men standing in front of him. She was passionate in bed, beautiful in her devotion to him.

"If she did …" He didn't know how to finish his sentence. He didn't know anything right now.

"She would have had a good reason," Rick said in a firm voice. Dom looked to him to see that he had already made up his mind. It didn't matter if she was or not. Rick was set that was she was still Alice to him.

Dominic wasn't so sure. He didn't know if he could continue with her in his life after a betrayal like that. He also knew that he couldn't live without her either. He couldn't picture the woman that he had spent so much time with being a spy. The two didn't mix. She would have to have put on an amazing act, and the thought alone left a bitter taste in his mouth.

He sighed, weariness beating at him from all sides, and patted Danny, who looked about as heartbroken as he was sure he did, on the shoulder before turning and walking silently into the room. Back to her room to resume his watch. He walked to the end of the bed, to the chair he sat in earlier. His thoughts were no less confusing than they were before, and he knew that it was going to be a long night.

Chapter 23

Alice jerked out of sleep with a cry, sitting straight up as the memories of the night before flew through her mind. She flinched as she remembered Dominic's face. She couldn't remember anything after that, though, and wondered if she had passed out. Tears leaked out of the corners of her eyes and she dropped her head down into her hands, taking deep breathes, trying not to let the pain and fear get to her.

She couldn't believe that Geo had worked for her uncle. That was almost more than she could deal with right now. She honestly didn't know what was worse. Her uncle being the head of the West Coast Crime Syndicate, or the fact that Dominic thought that she had betrayed him. Everything about them, their relationship, her loving him, it was all going down the drain. Even if he hadn't said that he loved her, she had thought that they had something real. That she could finally be free of the fear that followed her around constantly. None of that mattered now, though.

If he could believe that she did something like that, then nothing mattered anymore. She didn't know what to think, but what she did know was that she needed to leave. She would have to call Taby. She would help her. Then she would go back to her life, the way it seemed things were supposed to be.

She lifted her head, intent on finding her phone and calling Taby, when she saw Dominic sitting in the corner chair, staring at her. His normally dark eyes were glittering and his body was tense. His hair was sticking up as if he had run his fingers through it one too many times, and he had deep shadows under his eyes. She didn't know how long he had been there, but the fact that he would rather be across the room than in bed with her said it all. Things were over between them, and she would never be the same. She needed to draw up her courage and save the last little bit of her heart left.

"I need to make a call." She had to remember that she didn't owe him anything. He might have saved her from Boris and shown her that there could be more to life than what she had before, but everything else was a lie. He didn't believe in her, and he certainly didn't trust her.

"Why?" His words were low and tight. She thought of not answering him and just finding her phone on her own, but the Dominic she knew wouldn't let it drop.

"I'm calling Taby." She turned and searched the room and saw her purse and phone on the table. She got up, thankful that she was still wearing yesterday's clothes and that she wasn't naked. Going to her purse, she purposefully ignored Dom.

No, it was Dominic, she thought.

He wasn't her Dom anymore.

She grabbed her phone and then noticed that her purse was open and things were off. She always kept things in order so she could find them. It was one of her pet peeves.

Another shot of pain went through her at the thought that he had even gone through her purse. She shouldn't be surprised, but she was. She picked up the phone and started to dial Taby, when it was yanked out of her hand.

"Hey!" she cried out.

"We need to talk," he said while shoving her phone into his pocket.

"No, what you need to do is give me my phone so I can get out of here." She was starting to get mad. Why did stuff like this always happen to her? She hadn't ever done anything to deserve it, and she was getting tired of it.

"You know what, never mind." She grabbed her purse and walked into the closet to grab her book bag for school. Everything else she would leave; she didn't want anything that he had bought her anyway. It was too painful. She pushed those feelings aside and tried to go back to being mad. It would be a lot easier if she was mad.

She didn't get far. Grabbing her backpack, she turned around and walked right into Dominic's chest. His arms came up to steady her, but he didn't let go. His grip was hard and she knew that she was going to have bruises in the morning.

"Tell me it's not true." His words were harsh and abrasive, letting her see the pain and hurt in his eyes. Allowing her to see past the wall that he had placed between them, and it pissed her off even more. How dare he feel hurt.

He was the one who hadn't trusted her. He was the one who hadn't even asked her. He was the one who had believed that she was there to spy on him for a man she hated! Why couldn't he just trust her?

147

"Let me go." She tried to wiggle out of his grasp, but his grip tightened, and she flinched in pain.

"Tell me it's not true!" He was near shouting now.

"What? Tell you what?" she screamed back at him. Her fear was starting to come back, mixing with her anger, and it was swirling in her stomach. He had her cornered in the closet, a death grip on her arms, as she pushed against him, fighting to get free, but he wouldn't let go.

"Tell me you're not working for him! For Geo!" he snarled right back, his face so close to hers that she could feel him breathing. She tried to lean back away from him, but he had a death grip on her arm.

Then she felt it. Something that she hadn't ever felt before.

It was anger.

Red-hot, boiling anger.

It was shooting through her like fire flowing through a forest. Anger at her parents for leaving and her uncle for beating her. At Boris, Geo, Melissa, and even Dominic. Anger at all of it came shooting forward, filling her body.

Then she lost it.

Shoving him with a strength that she didn't know she had, he rocked back on one foot. One of his hands lost purchase on her arm, his other hand tightening. But she didn't feel that. All she felt was the anger, and right then it was aimed at Dominic.

"How dare you! How dare you!" She was screaming, a high pitch like she had never heard from herself before.

"How could you think that I would work for him! That I would work for that man!" She didn't register his face and how it was hard, his eyes glittered, she just kept going.

"You ass! I trusted you! I trusted you, and you think that I'm what? Some kind of whore that would sleep with you to get whatever answers I need to give to him? That I would what go back to him and let him beat me more before he sold me? That's why I left! And you, God, I trusted you, you asshole!" She was heaving as she watched his arm drop. He stepped back, horror swirling in his gaze.

It was at that look that she felt herself deflate. That was the look that she had never wanted to see from him. The horror over what had happened to her, and the guilt. She crossed her arms over her chest and looked to the floor, because looking at him hurt too much.

"Sweets." The words were spoken softly from the door to the closet, and both she and Dominic jumped, not knowing that anyone was there.

"Danny," she whispered in relief. Would he help her? Or did he think she was spying on them, too?

"Get out," Dominic whispered at Danny, but both he and Rick shook their heads.

"Get out!" Dom said again, harsher this time.

"Boss." This was from Danny and seemed to catch Dominic's attention. "Let us take this, okay?" Danny didn't give him a chance to respond, and instead stepped into the closet and wrapped his arm around her.

"Come on." She leaned into his embrace in relief. He might side with Dominic, but at least he was willing to help her out. She nearly cried when she realized that when she left she probably wouldn't be able to see him and Rick again.

They had become such a huge part of her, helping to build herself back up. They had become just as good of friends as

Taby and Troy. She couldn't picture what she would do without them making her laugh and just being there for her. Like they were now.

They walked her out of the closet and past Dominic, who looked like he didn't know what to do. Pain and anger were swirling around all of them, and when he caught her eye she saw the guilt. She couldn't handle that right now, so she looked away.

"Where are we going?" Her anger seemed to take everything out of her. She felt as if she hadn't slept in days, even if she did just wake up.

"We just have some questions." When she tensed at his words, he continued, "Shh. It's all right. We just need to figure out how this all goes together."

She figured that she didn't really have a choice, as they were both leading her to Dominic's office. Two other men stood at the doors, almost as guards, opening the door for them. Dominic came in behind them and she averted her gaze.

The sooner she got this done, the quicker she could get out of here, she thought.

She sat in one of the chairs and both Danny and Rick sat across from her on the couch. Dominic didn't sit down with them, and instead stayed by the doors. She tried not to let his distance hurt her; it was what she wanted after all, but it still hurt.

Danny laid a photo out in front of her and she flinched when she saw it was Geo. Stupid Geo. He was the one who had started all this. Then she thought better of it. *It was probably me actually*.

It was her hoping for more than what she had been given. As if she hadn't already learned her lesson the first time.

150

"I'm going to ask you a few things, Sweets, and I need you to answer honestly. It won't matter to me, okay? I just need the truth." He paused and looked at Dominic, then quickly continued.

"Then when we're done, I'll take you anywhere you want to go. Okay?" She knew instantly that Dominic wasn't happy with what he said, she could practically feel it behind her, but it wasn't his choice anymore. She knew that she was going to have to tell them everything, and this certainly wasn't the way she had wanted to do it. *But none of that mattered now*, she thought.

She nodded to them, nodding to them that she was ready.

"Had you met Geo before Dom?"

"No."

"Never? You never saw him or ran into him, anything like that?"

"No." He nodded at her answer then placed another photo down on the coffee table between them.

"How about him?" She took a deep breath and called on every ounce of strength that she had, trying to keep her voice from trembling when she spoke.

"Yes." Her voice wasn't as strong as she had hoped, but she continued anyway. "That's my uncle."

They didn't seem to be surprised, but they still paused and looked at each other.

"Did you live with him?" Memories were starting to flood her mind, the good and the bad, and all she could do was nod at him.

"Did you work for him?" She scowled as a deep weariness pushed at her. She wanted this whole thing to be over.

"No, I didn't work for him." She took a deep breath then told them the story of what had forever changed her life.

"My parents and I lived outside Houston. I was born there and lived there till I was thirteen. We were the traditional American family, I guess. A nice house, a dog, we even had a pool in the backyard. My mom was a first-grade teacher and my dad worked construction building homes. I remember watching them. It didn't matter where they were or what we were doing, but you could always tell that they loved each other. It was like a string was attached to each of them. I remember them dancing in the living room and teasing each other in the kitchen while my mom cooked. It was perfect." She looked out the window, the memories washing over her.

"One day for their anniversary, they decided to go on a vacation to the beach while I stayed with a friend. They were supposed to come home on Sunday night, but when it came and went I knew something was wrong. It wasn't until Monday evening that the sheriff finally came to tell us that they had been in a car crash. They both died instantly."

"Shit." She didn't look up at Rick's words, just smiled a small sad smile and continued her story.

"I was placed in a group home for a while, cause as far as we knew neither of my parents had family. Then one day about a month later this man shows up. He looked just like my dad, except he had reddish-brown hair and my dad had thick black hair. I had always, for as long as I can remember, wished that I had gotten my dad's hair," she said as she remembered her father teasing her about her brown wavy locks that looked like her mother's.

"Anyways, the man said that he hadn't kept in touch and had just heard the news. It wasn't long before he had custody, and we moved to Seattle where he lived. At first, it was okay. I had my own room and really didn't come out that much. It was probably as if I wasn't even there. Then the summer ended and I had to go to school. It became a hassle for him and he became vocal about how he didn't like that it was taking up his time, driving me around, and that I was in his way."

She paused. She really didn't want to continue this, to share this part of her life.

"Go on, Sweets," Danny said softly.

"Anyways, partway through the school year he decided to homeschool me. He filed everything and then it was just no more school." She shrugged. "I guess that's when things started to change. He didn't have to hide things anymore. He moved me down to the basement and out of my room, and ... things, well, got bad after that."

"What did he do?" was spoken slowly and with an air of menace from Dominic. She looked up to see that he had come farther into the room and was standing closer to her chair. She turned back around and kept her gaze on her lap, she couldn't finish this if she was looking at him. "He would hit me, take away meals. I tried to escape one day. But he caught me and then he chained the door, locking me down there. I guess I was lucky he didn't ever let his men rape me, like he threatened." The men in the room all cursed, but she kept her head down. Talking about her past was harder than she thought it would be, especially now.

"When I turned eighteen he kept talking about how much money I was going to make him. At first, I didn't know what to think. Then one day I was up in the house, making food for him and some of his guys, when I overheard them saying how much they could get for me. They were saying things like auction, and girls, and it freaked me out. Things started to make

153

sense and that night I decided to ask my uncle about it. I had this stupid idea in my head that he would somehow help me, and that it wasn't really what I'd heard. That he wouldn't do that to me. But he just told me that it was true. That he was going to sell me to the highest bidder. Said that the money would be his way in and that he hoped that whoever got me made it hurt." She was crying now, remembering his words and the cruel smile that he had given her. Her breathing was fast and she felt light-headed. She hated remembering that time in her life.

"Breathe, Sweets." Danny came closer to her and kneeled in front of her.

"With me." He mimicked breathing in and out slowly so she would follow him. Soon it helped and she felt semi normal again. She gave him a small nod of thanks and continued.

"I ran," she forced out, needing them to know what had happened. Afterwards, she could get away to curl up and cry her heart out, but she had to finish this. Dominic was standing over her shoulder, and it made her nervous. She wondered what he thought of her now that he knew everything, but she was just too tired to care.

"One day I received paperwork about my parents' trust fund. The lady who cleaned the house was there. She helped me escape. It was pure luck that nobody was home. That I was even able to sneak out, but it was my chance, so I took it. I ran and I didn't look back. I went to shelters and they helped me get out of the state. Later I found myself here. By then I hadn't seen him around or heard anything and I figured he hadn't cared as much as I thought. I got my trust fund and started school, got a job, and never looked back."

"If you had a trust fund why were you living in that shithole that we found you in?" She jumped at Dom's voice and

Danny shot him a glare. Anger and embarrassment over her apartment shot through her. How dare he ask her that! She could hardly stand to look at him when she answered.

"I didn't have much. Just enough to pay for my tuition and some of my books. I worked to pay for my apartment and everything else."

They were silent afterward. She, however, felt numb, the whole thing having taken its toll. Alice slowly felt her body start to sag as the day started to catch up with her. She needed to call Taby and get out of here before she fell apart.

"Can I go?"

"Boss?" Rick was giving Dom a look that she couldn't read. They stared at each other for a few minutes.

She looked back and forth between them, hoping for any answer to her question. Hoping that they would let her go now. When Danny squeezed her knee affectionately and stood, nudging Rick, she knew that they were leaving her with Dominic. One part of her, mostly her heart, was hopeful that they could still figure this out and they would be okay. Her head, on the other hand, was telling her to run. That he hadn't trusted her the first time and she needed to protect herself.

"It's fine, man. They need to work this out." Danny's words were confident, but the look he sent Dominic had a hard edge to it. Even now she still didn't like that she had come between them all. To her, they had both become cherished friends, but to Dominic, they were family.

Rick seemed to stare Dominic down for another second, then nodded and walked out of the room. Danny followed him, turning to give her a last look over his shoulder as he left.

She wanted to call out not to leave her. To plead for them to take her with them. But she knew at that moment that they were siding with Dominic. She couldn't fault them that. She was the outsider, after all.

Chapter 24

Dominic kneeled in front of her and grasped her hands in his. They stared at their joined hands; she didn't know how to feel. She was so conflicted. How he had acted scared her, reminding her of her uncle. Then there was the trust that she had been starting to build, which was now badly shaken.

She knew that she couldn't place all the blame on him, though. If she had told him about her past earlier, then he wouldn't have come to the conclusions that he had. She could have prevented this.

Sure, there might have still been some confusion, but it wouldn't have left her feeling like their trust had been frayed. She knew that she needed to own up to her mistake, but even then she didn't know if there was anything they could do to fix what had been done.

If she could have learned to trust him, then she knew without a doubt that he would have trusted her. It was just the man that he was.

"Sweetheart, look at me." His voice was soft and gentle in a way that she hadn't ever heard from him before. It was almost as if he was begging.

"Please." This time he was begging, and it did her in. Tears rolling down her cheeks, she glanced up and gasped at the sight of his watery eyes.

"I'm sorry I didn't tell you," she whispered, her only hope that they could rebuild what they had.

"I knew that it was going to be bad, how hesitant you were with me when you first came here, and the way that you didn't want to open up to me. But I never would have imagined this." He took a deep breath. "We couldn't figure out Geo's insider connection. We thought that maybe it was Brittany."

She remembered the woman in his office had seemed to set him off. But now that she knew the connection, things made a bit more sense.

"Some of my men started to question that you came into my life right at the time that Geo went down. It's been a fucking mess trying to tie up all the loose ends from leaving the Familia, and I didn't want to believe that you would do something like that. But I didn't want to go in blind again. I trusted Geo and everyone he hired. I followed them, blindly trusting in their loyalty to me and the Familia, and it turned out to cost me more than just money." His tone was desperate, and his eyes were staring deep into her. As if he was trying to get her to believe him. It wasn't that she didn't believe him, she just didn't know how to get past it.

"I made a mistake, sweetheart. They were telling me this stuff in that meeting, then you walked in and were right in front of me." He let her hands go and shoved them through his hair.

"I didn't have time to process anything, and I had so many thoughts running through my head, and I kept saying to myself that I didn't know you, you hadn't opened up yet. That you hadn't even been here that long. I'm not telling you this because I want an excuse, I'm just trying to get you to understand where my head was at." Silently he grabbed her hand in a desperate grip and just sat there with her as she worked through her thoughts.

She knew that some of this was her fault. Even if her heart was hurt because of his actions, she couldn't blame him for everything. She needed to take responsibility for her actions.

"I should have told you," she whispered.

The circle of should-haves was going wild in her mind and she was overcome with another wave of exhaustion. Dominic must have noticed, as he reached forward and cupped her cheek with one hand. Then in one motion he scooped her up and walked them to his couch. Laying her down with her head pillowed in his lap, he ran his hand through her hair, pulling her into a sleepy trance.

"Sleep, sweetheart," he whispered, pulling her close to his body as if to never let her go. She loved the feeling of his arms around her, but this time it was contradicting. How could she sleep when there was still so much unsaid between them? But as soon as the thought came, she was out.

***

Dominic lay on the couch in his office, watching Alice sleep. It was still relatively early in the morning. Their fight had lasted late into the night, into the early hours of the morning before she had fallen asleep on his lap. He of course couldn't sleep.

His mind kept going over the many different things that he should have done differently. Wishes and wants, but it didn't matter. He had been given a lot in his life, and he had a lot to be thankful for. His family had always made it known that he would never have to blindly follow his family's ways. That he was free to choose his own way. It had cost his family a lot for them to give that to him, and although he knew that they would do it again he was still very ashamed of himself.

He had taken everything that he had been given and taken it for granted. Hearing her story and about her life made him realize that he hadn't had to really fight for one single thing to leave the Familia. His father had done most of the work. Something almost unheard of. And yet, while he was given such a gift, she was out there fighting for her life. Scraping by to be better. When had he ever worked that hard for a necessity? He knew now that he had a lot to make up for.

He thought again of a new start, the idea that had once filtered through his mind. The idea had more merit now. The ability to give her that, a fresh start wherever she wanted. He wouldn't necessarily need to go south toward one of his clubs, he could easily take her anywhere she wanted to go.

That was if she decided to stay with him. It was a hard pill for him to swallow, thinking that after all that they had gone through, making this life together, he might have screwed up enough to make her walk. He grimaced at the thought.

She stirred, a small sigh escaping her mouth. He watched as her fingers flexed and she slowly came awake. Each little thing he tried to memorize, every movement about her, knowing that it could be his last time to watch her wake up. He knew that he would fight for her like he had never fought for anything else. He just hoped that he was enough.

Her eyes opened and he watched as they filtered from sleepy to confusion. They flickered around the room till they landed on him. They sat there staring at each other and he watched as sadness, then hope, slowly shown in her eyes, and he wondered if his were mirroring the same. His chest ached with so much unresolved between them.

He let his fingers slide through her hair, letting its silkiness slip through, but he kept his eyes on hers, never looking away. If these were to be some of his last moments with her, he didn't want to miss any of it.

A deep sigh came from her, but he couldn't tell what it meant. He was building up the courage to say something—what, he didn't know—but she spoke first.

"Can we go somewhere today?" Her words were slight and frail, and he hated hearing it in her voice. She was changing the topic. Veering away from their troubles. Although the agony of not knowing was haunting him, he gladly would jump at the chance to put the conversation on hold.

"Where?" Little did she know that he would take her anywhere.

"Anywhere. I just want to get away today. Just you and me." She blushed.

*Probably at her word*s, he thought, but she couldn't have known the feelings coursing through him. Joy that she wanted to spend the day with him and hope that it could be a chance to fix this. Even determination, because he had learned from an early age not to ever give up. He smiled at the thought.

No, he wasn't ever going to give up.

"I know just the place." He drew her up with him and headed to their room to pack, his mind working overtime on a plan. He would give her today, mostly because that's what she had asked for but also because he wanted it just as much.

Chapter 25

It wasn't long before they were on the road. He had thought about taking his vintage convertible, but the weather still wasn't warm enough. However, the thought of rolling down the highway with her hair blowing out behind her was something that he was going to put on his to-do list.

For now, though, it was enough to see her relaxed as she watched the scenery go by. He had opted for the small highway instead of the larger freeway. It was something that he had grown to love, the feeling of leaving the city behind, and he hoped that it would make her feel better as well.

It was an odd feeling, thinking of someone else's welfare for once. For so long he didn't really have a purpose. Sure, he built up his nightclubs spanning several states, and for the last several years he had helped his father figure out the Familia business. But he had never really given any thought to anything beyond that. That all changed when he saw her. He remembered asking her what she had wanted out of life that one afternoon at the little diner downtown. Maybe it was time that he started asking himself that as well.

"If you could go anywhere, where would it be?" She surprised him with the question. He glanced at her to see her still turned toward the window, and wondered if she had been thinking about the same thing he had.

After a few seconds of thought he answered, even surprising himself.

"Florida. I wanted to go to school there, but instead I ended up going locally. My grandfather lived there though for a short time. It was where he met my grandmother."

"I didn't know that. You don't talk about your family much." She was looking at him now, and he could see the curious expression on her beautiful face. It gave him a bit of hope.

"I guess I haven't, have I? My grandfather was never happy with his lot in life. Having to take over the Familia and lead. Back then it was more ... gruesome and gritty, I guess you could say. He lived in a little town in Italy, and back then it was Familia or death. He didn't really have a choice." He told her a bit of his history, while reaching over to squeeze her hand.

"Anyway, he got the chance to come to America through one of the Bosses. It was a great honor that not very many were offered. He used to go on and on about the honor, but he hated it all the same. Once he met my grandmother and they started a family, he knew that he could never force his children to make the same sacrifices that he had. However, it was not that easy to just leave. It would take generations, and my father would finally complete it. They gave up everything for me. My father sold everything in payment to the local boss, Ivanov, so that I could live this life. I have a lot to be thankful for."

Even you, he silently added.

***

Alice could hear the emotion running through his voice. He had told her little bits of his past here and there, but never had he spoken with such depth of emotion. She reached over and grasped his hand, holding it tightly between them.

She knew that he was silently berating himself for his part in their fight yesterday, but what he didn't realize was that she was doing the same thing. She woke up this morning with a need to make him understand that she could not leave. It would break her. Just like she knew that it would break him. She wanted them to have a future, they just both had to work on their communication. Easier said than done, but if they wanted it bad enough they could make it work.

"You haven't ever mentioned your father before."

"He's in Europe now, with his wife. He went back to Italy for a time."

"Do you not like his new wife?" she asked. It made her sad to know that he hadn't been able to grow up with his mother. The irony wasn't lost on her though. They had both lost a parent when they were young.

"She's okay. For as long as I can remember growing up, my father never had anyone. He focused on me and the Familia. I think my mother being killed was harder on him than he let on. But after I was grown he started to see people on occasion, although he always kept it very low-key. Last year he met this woman. Normal, like you." She scoffed at that. "They were married in Italy after he left. Said he wanted to start fresh, wouldn't marry her until he was officially out."

"Can he not come back here?" She loved that he was opening up to her.

"He can but not easily, and not for a bit. His power here makes him a target. Also, he was just as hungry for this to be over as I think my grandfather was. He deserves a break." His voice was firm and she knew that, while he probably missed his father, they were all glad as a family to be able to live their own lives.

"I'll take you there someday." She could tell that he was a bit uncertain, and he glanced out of the corner of his eye to watch her reaction.

"Anytime, anywhere, Dominic." Her tone quiet, but strong. She loved this man with everything in her. How that happened over such a short time she didn't know, but it was no less true. It seemed like she had something to be thankful for, too.

The car pulled sharply to the side and she gasped, thinking that something was wrong. He shifted it to park and turned toward her, his gaze searing her with emotion.

"You mean that." His voice floated over her as his hand reached up to her cheek, and she saw the slight tremble it had to it.

"Yes."

"Even after yesterday." She knew that he was uncertain, and a little afraid of her telling him no. She was scared of the same thing, but he didn't have to worry. She felt the same as him. Desperate to not let go.

The 'yes' was hardly out of her mouth before he was pulling her into his kiss. His lips moving over hers, his tongue brushed over where his teeth nibbled and bit. It was passionate, it was teasing, and it was filled with hope.

She knew then that everything was going to be okay.

***

He sat on the edge of the lake, watching her splash in the shallows. Her hair was bouncing around her shoulders, shining in the sun. She had her pants rolled up, and although he knew the water had to be pretty cold it didn't look to be bothering her at all. He was enjoying sitting there, watching her. In this moment she was carefree. He had seen her grow over the last few months and loved seeing her come alive.

Yesterday had been a setback, no doubt about it. His stupidity could have cost him something that was so precious to him. Something that deserved to be treasured. After their talk in the car, he had found himself opening up and really talking to her. He had found out a lot more about her past and had shared just as much. It had felt good to talk to her. I had felt right.

He could see what his grandfather and father had been talking about, finding something to love and following his own path. He had found his. It was her. He could see them sitting on a front porch with their kids playing in the yard. Every night with her lying next to him till the day he died. That was what he wanted.

His mood dipped as he thought about what awaited them when they got home. They still hadn't found Geo, and now he needed to worry about the connection that Alice had to the West Coast Capo. He wondered if he should call his father and ask his opinion.

Technically Dominic wasn't Familia anymore, neither was his father, so dealing with all this was not going to be easy. He had a clean break from all this, and involving them all in that life again was a dangerous move. He had never wanted to just up and leave more than he did right now. He knew, though, that leaving wouldn't solve his problems.

There was Alice to consider, too. Would she even be willing to leave? He knew that she wouldn't want to leave Taby behind, but that was her only real connection to this place. He had the thought that maybe he could get Taby and Troy to come with them. He knew that Troy was having a hard time, but if Troy would take his help maybe they could get him set up somewhere. Although Dominic wasn't sure if he would. He had tried to help him before.

He watched her wander up to him and smiled a little at the open joy on her face. He loved that about her, how she wasn't afraid to wear her heart on her sleeve. She sat down next to him, looking out over the lake. The day was ending, and the sun was just starting to set. He needed to be open with her. As open as she was with him.

"Would you go with me if I was to move?"

"What do you mean, like houses?" Her brow was scrunched up in the cutest way, and it made him smile. She was so beautiful in everything she did, even when her face was all scrunched up and confused. He didn't think she would want to hear it, though.

"No. I meant someplace different." He paused, then decided to go for broke.

It was trust.

It was building something more.

A future.

"Part of the deal with signing over our territory and local business holdings was that we had to give up certain things. For my father, it was his connections and all the debts owed to him. He handed them over for the new boss to take. For me, it was my clubs here. I wasn't that financially diverse in the Familia's holdings, but I still signed over a large percentage, broke up the chain, and only retained ownership of the clubs that are out of state. With that, I don't really have a reason to stay here beyond you."

"You can't stay?" she whispered, looking sad.

"Way I figure it, if I could talk Taby and Troy into going down South to where some of my clubs are, maybe I could help them out as well. Maybe find Troy a good job. What else would you need for me to get you to follow?" he finished, and watched her face transform with a smile.

"We could pick anywhere. I don't have to be in one location. And anytime I'm needed we can just fly there for a few days. Where would you want to go? Maybe somewhere where it's warmer?"

"Florida," she said with no hesitation. He watched her smile get even bigger, and a warm feeling filled him at the gift that he was given in her.

"Yeah, I can do that." His voice was soft as he cupped her chin and kissed her nose. Watching the blush spread over her face, he knew that he was right where he wanted to be.

"Okay, baby. Now that that's settled, give me a real kiss." She wrapped her arms around his neck, giggling, and kissed him like she loved him.

She did, he said to himself.

Chapter 26

Three Months Later

Alice couldn't believe that she was graduating.

It had been almost ten months since she met Dominic, and her life couldn't have been any better. The only dark spot was that Dominic was out of town, so she had stayed at Taby and Troy's house last night. She missed him, but it had been nice to catch up with her friends.

The last few months had been so busy, her getting ready to graduate and Dominic finishing up things with his business. Then, on top of everything, Dominic was still moving in a couple of weeks.

Or, she should say, *they* were moving.

She was having mixed feelings about it really. Troy and Taby hadn't wanted to go. Taby only had a couple more years left to go of school and Troy had finally just gotten a job. They had both said maybe later, but right now wasn't the best timing. She could understand it, but it still made the decision to move difficult. Dominic, understanding as ever, said it was up to her.

In the end, she had decided that although they were her friends, she was choosing a life with Dominic. They needed this fresh start. Besides, she could always come and visit.

She was just glad that Danny and Rick had decided to come. Rick was taking the head of security position at Dominic's new clubs. Danny was staying on and taking over as their head of personal security. With Dominic's past they would still need some personal security around them at all times, and probably always would.

The last few months had been so great for her and Dominic. They had both decided that communication was so important to their future. They had seen a small glimpse of what their future looked like without each other, and neither one of them would ever do anything to jeopardize that again. Alice was more open with her past, and although it wasn't easy to talk about it at first it soon became easier. Dominic did the same, talking about his day and all his troubles, including not being able to find Geo.

Remaining an open book for her.

That was the only blight on their otherwise great last few months. Geo was nowhere to be found. Dominic, of course, was sure that he was just waiting in the shadows for another chance. But as time went on Alice was starting to think that he wasn't here at all and had taken off. She wondered if he had gone back to the West Coast.

Dominic had petitioned the boss here in town. Both of them would be having a meeting with the head of the West Coast chapter next week.

Her uncle.

She was terrified as to what was going to happen. But Dominic seemed sure that everything was going to go just fine.

He kept telling her that with everybody there he wouldn't pull anything.

Once they had gotten home from their little day trip, he had immediately started putting out feelers about her uncle and her connection to the West Coast. Needless to say, Dominic was not happy to find out that it hadn't been any help. None of them had heard from Geo. And as for her uncle, he couldn't care less. Supposedly.

She was still suspicious. It all seemed to be too much of a coincidence. Dominic had told her that when they had a phone meeting with her uncle, he had seemed surprised that she was even alive.

There wasn't any joyous reunion and he seemed to not care that she was alive or not, but Dom was thinking that he wasn't a big worry. That he was content to rule his nest from his perch far away from them. It was something that she didn't think she would ever stop worrying about.

She also worried that Dominic wouldn't be able to let it go. What happened to her at times seemed to eat at him. He would often brush it off, but she knew that the type of man that he was. It was very unlikely that he was just going to let it go.

Checking her watch, she saw that it was almost time to go. Taking one last look in the mirror she headed out to the front of the house, where Taby and Troy were waiting on her.

She tried to not let Dominic's absence get to her. He had said that he was going to be back yesterday, but his plans had been delayed due to a big storm over the Gulf Coast. She wasn't sure who was more disappointed, her or Dominic. She knew that this meeting was important and that he hadn't wanted to go without her. She just missed him and was sad that he wasn't going to be here today.

"YOU READY?" Taby squealed so loud that both she and Troy rubbed their ears. "I can't believe it! I'm so proud of you!" Taby rushed forward and gripped her in a rib-cracking hug.

She didn't mind, she could hardly believe it either. She had made it! Her feelings about today were so contradicting. Happy to have completed this accomplishment for not only her parents but also herself. She was also overcome with a feeling of sadness, and a tear leaked down her cheek.

"Hey there, girl, what's all this?" Troy asked, walking toward her after seeing her face. She drew back from Taby and gave them a small smile.

"For so long all I've thought about is finishing school and making them proud. To do something with myself, like they wanted me to. But now that I've done it feel kind of like I lost them all over again."

"Come here, girl." Troy drew her toward him and placed his hands on her shoulders as he spoke.

"You are one of the strongest people that I know. The things that you have overcome, that is why your parents would be proud of you. Sure, going to school and finishing is great, it is. Taby and I are proud of you for that, too."

"But knowing just a little of what you have endured in your life? That, Alice, is why they are proud of you." All she could do was give him a smile through her tears.

"You know he's right, doll." At the sound of Rick's voice, they all turned to see Danny and Rick standing there, with smiles on their faces.

"And it's about time you knew it, too!" Danny bellowed. He was so loud that all the neighboring apartments probably

172

heard him. They all smiled at him and his always present boisterous attitude.

"Come on! My cameras all charged up and we are not going to miss this!" Taby dramatically gestured, and the men just shook their heads at her. Alice smiled and headed out the door.

Taby was right, *she wasn't going to miss this.*

***

"Alice Beckman."

Alice walked up the steps onto the stage, following the person in front of her. Her heart was racing and all she could think about at that moment was to not trip and fall. She could hear Taby and the others shouting in the stands.

Several of Dominic's men had shown up to offer their support to her, and she had been so touched. Even if she had only met some of them a couple of times, that they were there for her meant more to her than anything. Dominic was still not answering his phone. She had tried to call him right before she went on stage, but there was no answer.

Danny had tried to reassure her that he was trying to get home, but she couldn't help but feel a little upset that he wasn't here for this. She pushed those thoughts aside as she accepted her degree and shook hands with her former professors. She smiled out toward the audience as she heard Taby scream out.

"Way to go, Alice!" Alice could just make out the sight of her jumping up and down, waving her arms around in the stands. Troy, standing behind, was holding on to her as if trying to keep her from jumping out of the stands, a big smile on his face.

She glanced down as she walked down the stairs, making sure to watch her step. When she reached the bottom, she almost ran into a man standing there.

"Oh! Excuse …" Her voice trailed off as she saw Dominic standing there, with a bouquet of flowers and a smile on his handsome face.

"You made it!" she cried out as she flung herself toward him. He caught her up in a hug so tight she almost couldn't breathe, but she didn't care. She was just so happy that he was there.

"I'm sorry I'm so late. I couldn't find a plane," he whispered into her hair.

"It's okay. You're here, that's all that matters," she babbled through her tears. She drew back to tell him that again and gasped as she saw his face. She lightly cupped the side of his face in horror, looking at a huge bruise. He grasped her shoulders gently.

"It's okay, baby. It was worth it."

"Does it hurt?" she whispered.

"No." His answer was steady. But she wasn't sure if she believed him.

"Come on, I believe there is a celebration planned for you." He drew her in front of him and leaned down to whisper in her ear again.

"You and I will celebrate later." She knew that he was trying to distract her, as his hand on her side slid up and his thumb brushed against the underside of her breast. Yes, she was looking forward to tonight, and to figuring out what had happened with Dom.

Chapter 27

"Yes, please. Please," she moaned as she pushed her hips up toward him, trying to get him deeper inside of her.

His slow teasing was driving her mad and she needed to come desperately. He had spent the last couple of hours touching every part of her body.

Slowly, gently driving her mad.

He would drive in deep, only to pull out and go back down on her. Every time she got close, he would pull away. She didn't think that she was going to survive this much longer.

"Dom, please." Her voice cracked and she arched up again. Her hands reached down to his head and she pulled at his hair in desperation.

"Not yet, baby," he said, licking his wet lips. He drew up, grabbing her wrists and holding them in place above her head. She arched up into him as he came up over her, laying kisses on her stomach as he moved. She wiggled under him, her body unable to stay still much longer, and heard him chuckle.

He leaned over the edge of the bed and grabbed his tie. Her breath stalled as he gently wrapped it around her wrists, overlapping it so it wasn't putting pressure on one single spot but was still secure. Reaching over her head, he tied the ends to the headboard.

"Good?" he questioned, looking at her. She gave an experimental tug that had him chuckling and frustration filling her. She could get out if she wanted to, but it would take a bit of pulling. It didn't matter, though. She was so needy for him and he knew it, keeping her on the edge.

"Let's see you stop me now." His words whispered in her ear as he kissed his way back down her body, only adding to the flames of desire that she was drowning in.

"Enjoy your present, baby." His head dipped between her thighs and then he was licking her, devouring her. Her attention fractured as he went back to work, driving her mad.

They'd had a wonderful dinner with everybody who had come to her graduation and then made their way home. She had planned to ask him about his bruise, but the minute they made it through the door he had been on her. Pressing her against the door with his body, she had instantly forgotten everything else.

Now she was tied to the bed, a mass of nerves, on the edge. Every kiss and touch sent a wave of fire through her, her body a never-ending ball of sensation that only he could control.

She loved it.

"Please …" She was begging now and didn't care one bit. She would do anything at this point to get him to let her come. His mouth suckled at her clit in gentle pulls.

Never enough to give her what she really needed.

"What do you want?" he questioned in a husky voice. As if he didn't already know.

"Please! I want to come, anything, just please!" Her voice sounded needy and desperate even to her. Her hips bucked against him as he left his position, sliding his thigh between her legs. His hands at her hips guided her movements as she rubbed herself against him.

"Christ, you are so fucking beautiful. That's it, baby, fuck yeah." His words were starting to shorten. His breathing coming in shorter pants, her effect on him just as dangerous.

"Not yet, baby." He suddenly pulled away, and she cried out in disappointment.

"No! Please! Why?" She didn't really expect an answer, just arched and moaned as he came up over her again, aligning their bodies. Laying kisses along her neck, his hand trailed down to leave a trail of fire as he slowly circled her clit with his finger. Just enough to fly her higher, but still not enough, only to draw away again.

Her broken cry made him chuckle, and she lost it. She didn't care what his plan was anymore, all she could feel was this devastating need that only he could fill. Pulling and twisting her hands, she yanked herself free with desperate movements. She shoved him off her and used her newly unbound hands to climb over him. She didn't see him smile or grab her hips, urging her on and steading her.

She was lost in the pleasure.

He was so hard that he was sticking straight up as if waiting for her, and she sank down on him in one thrust. A sigh left her as she finally felt herself filled full. With him. Her hips started moving, her head thrown back.

"Fuck, baby," he muttered, but she was gone. Waves of it crashing over her as she came. Fire flowing through her, she screamed out as the strongest orgasm of her life crashed over her.

She was shaking and her vision was slightly hazy as she started to come down, when he turned the tables on her. Rolling them so she was under him, he started pounding into her at a furious pace, his control lost.

"That was so fucking hot, baby." She gasped as his thrusts became erratic and even faster than before, leaving her breathless in his passion.

She watched as his control slipped and that frantic desire took over. His hands grasping in wild abandon. Not able to get enough. His deep groan signaled that he was finally at his own peak and she watched as it came over him. A look of near pain crossing his face. Sheer rapture filled her as she felt his release, triggering one last ripple of pleasure through her body. His head dropped down into the curve of her shoulder and he nuzzled her.

"Look at me." His voice was soft and gentle as they both came down from their high.

"Do you love me?" he questioned, his hand coming up to gently grasp her neck. To focus her attention on him, as if it could be anywhere else.

"Yes, Dom. Yes, I love you." His gaze was searing, blazing through her. His heart flayed open for her.

"I'm not good with words. It's not my strong suit. My father was a great dad, but he never talked. Emotions were not something he was good with, he couldn't be. With the Familia, you didn't show weakness. Not even with the people closest to you. But you?" His pause was torture for both of them, and his eyes closed. Squeezing as if in pain. He seemed to gather himself, his eyes opening back on her.

"I know with every fiber of my being, I love you." His words were strong and sure. Never wavering. Just like him.

She let it flow over her, knowing that she would give everything she had to keep this.

Chapter 28

"Are you going to tell me what happened?" They were sitting at the table, eating breakfast. Alice had woken up to the smell of food and had rolled over to find no Dominic in the bed next to her. The night before flittered through her mind and she smiled, till she remembered that she hadn't gotten around to asking him about his bruises.

Now that she thought about it, she remembered seeing more on his chest. She rolled out of bed, snagging his shirt off the floor.

Dom had been in the kitchen with containers of food in bags around him, a sheepish look on his face.

"I wanted to cook for you, but honestly I can't cook, so …" He had trailed off with a shrug, and she had giggled. There was enough food for ten people. He really was cute when he was trying to make her happy and going overboard.

"Finish your breakfast first, then I'll tell you." His look said that he wasn't going to budge on this one at all.

"Is it that bad?" she whispered, sudden dread filling her. Their easygoing morning was suddenly covered in a cloud of anxiety. He gave her a glance that she thought looked a lot like sympathy.

"Please, baby, just finish." She took only a couple more bites and then set her fork down. There was no way she could eat now, and most of the plate had been cleared anyway.

"Okay." His voice was resigned. He pushed their dishes to the side and reached for her hands across the bar that they were sitting at.

"Please just tell me. Are you okay?" The thought instantly scared her that maybe he was in trouble. "Is it you? You're all right, right?" Her voice was rising and on the verge of becoming shrill. The thought that something was wrong with him hadn't even crossed her mind.

"Shh. Yes, I'm fine. Okay, I'll just do this fast." When she shakily nodded, he continued.

"Your uncle is dead." She blinked at him, not knowing how to respond to that. It certainly wasn't the news that she thought he would say. The news didn't hit her like she thought it would.

In fact, it didn't hit her at all.

"What?"

"He died of a heart attack. Nothing bad at all. I was on my way to talk to him …"

"WHAT? We were going to talk to him next week!" She couldn't keep up with him. What was going on?

"I know, but I got to thinking about it and I just didn't trust it. It didn't seem right to walk you right to him. But it doesn't matter. I got about halfway there and got the news."

"A heart attack?" she questioned. Her uncle hadn't been super unhealthy but, then again, she wasn't sure that she had paid that much attention.

"Yes. We haven't heard anything else." His voice held a tone that she wasn't sure about, but she decided to let it go.

"Are you okay?" She turned to see a frown on his face at his question.

"I know it sounds weird, and maybe it will hit me later, but I don't feel anything. Is that weird? I mean, he was horrible to me and never was any kind of family, and I was lucky to have just gotten out. But no, I don't feel anything. I guess at this point, it's just news."

"Come here, sweetheart." He stood and drew her into his arms. "It's not weird, baby. I don't think it will hit you till later. But you're right. If it never hits you then that's okay, too. All that matters is that he's gone." She let his arms comfort her as she snuggled into his embrace just a little bit more.

"I love you," she whispered into his chest.

"I love you, too." She would never get used to hearing that from him.

"Okay buster, that didn't answer my question! What does all this have to do with your face?"

"Let's just say that I had a difference of opinion with someone."

"Nope." She shook her head and stepped back, crossing her arms over her chest. "That's not going to do it. Tell me." He chuckled at her antics.

"There are a lot of people who wanted him dead, baby, and I was one of them. I was questioned. That's all." Her arms dropped and she stared at him, horrified.

"You mean my uncle's men did this?"

"It wasn't that bad. They quickly figured out that I'm not in that circle anymore. They were under the opinion that Geo was still working for me. Apparently, Geo was next in line, and we aren't the only ones who can't find him."

"So, my uncle didn't have anything to do with Geo stealing from you then."

"It's looking that way, yes. It could be that they kept it close to the vest and his lieutenants didn't know, but I doubt it." His arms drew her back to him and she leaned against him once more.

"So, what is Geo doing now? He can't access all the money he took from you, can he?" She shifted and moved back into his arms.

"No, it's no longer where they can reach it."

"Do you think they left? Like ran away?" He smiled down at her.

"Yeah baby, they probably ran away." But his eyes held something else. Something that slithered down her spine.

"What is it?" she whispered in concern. He looked away from her and over her shoulder, avoiding her gaze. He never did that.

"Dominic?" she pleaded. "Please, we promised to be honest with each other."

Her voice cracked; she knew that he was trying to protect her, but she also needed to know what was going on. She needed to be able to stand by him through thick and thin. To trust that he would give her everything. He needed to trust that she could take it. His shoulders seemed to droop a little at her words and he hugged her a little tighter.

"You've been getting letters. I didn't want to tell you. You had graduation and we were packing and trying to find a new house. I wanted you to concentrate on the future and not whatever this is supposed to be." He ran his fingers through his hair in frustration.

"Fuck!" His outburst startled her, and he apologized by rubbing his hands up her arms.

"What kind of letters?" His look confirmed her suspicion that they weren't good.

"What did they say?"

"Just warning you to leave, consequences if you don't. Nothing you need to worry about, okay?" His look was so imploring that she felt her resolve weaken. He was always so concerned with her.

When was he going to start looking out for himself, she wondered.

"That's confusing." Why would someone be telling her to leave?

"I know, baby. But I have this, okay? Just let me take care of this. I need you to not worry about it. Okay?" Dom drew her in closer and leaned down to kiss her neck.

She knew that she should probably fight him on this. Ask him more about what the letters said. But his voice had sounded so sincere, and she was just happy that they were talking about it, that she let it go.

"Okay. I will. But you can't keep me in the dark. Okay?" His sweet kiss was her answer.

"HEY!" She drew back, placing her hands on his chest. "Was that why all of a sudden you went to see my uncle?" The pieces were starting to come together now.

"Yes, and no. I wanted to know his feelings about you leaving, too."

"Oh …"

"That's enough. I have this, right?" At her nod, he continued. "You are supposed to be celebrating today. Taby is going to be here in about an hour, you girls are going out to do … whatever you girls do." She giggled at his befuddled look, and he smiled at her.

"Go get ready."

"Are you not going to come to get ready with me? Maybe you could help me wash my back." She whispered huskily, smoothing her hands up and down his chest, looking up at him from under her lashes.

He growled into her neck and she laughed as he swung her up in his arms and ran down the hallway, her laughter ringing after them.

Chapter 29

"Taby, that is ridiculous!" Alice laughed at her. She was sitting in the salon chair, getting her first pedicure. It was weird having someone paint her toes, but it also felt awesome.

"It is not! Troy told me I was crazy. Well, I'll show him crazy." She huffed in indignation.

"By painting your toes with 'fuck U' on them?" Alice laughed out. She was definitely feeling sorry for Troy right about now. He was not going to be getting any loving tonight.

"Serves him right." Taby looked every bit the pouting woman that she was. It made it hard for her to keep a straight face.

"What exactly did he do?" Alice was having a hard time not laughing.

"I don't want to talk about it!" she said haughtily.

"Uh-huh." This time Alice did laugh.

"It's not funny!" But even Taby was laughing now.

"Come on, tell me. Oh, poor Troy."

"Poor Troy!" Taby screeched. Alice couldn't hold it in any longer. She busted out laughing so hard the nail technician gave her a funny look.

"He told me if I got any crazier that I'd kill him."

"Kill him?" Alice choked out through her laughter, and Taby's cheeks went pink, which sent Alice into another round of laughter.

"You were in bed!" she accused.

"Shut up!" Taby pouted, with a smile though.

Once they were done with their nails, they walked down the street toward the coffee shop, while Taby continued to look over their shoulders at the men who were following them.

"Why do you have so many guards?"

She hesitated. She didn't want to keep anything from Taby, but she also didn't want to worry her.

"There's just some stuff going on. Dom just wants to make sure everything is safe."

"Where are Danny and Rick?"

"They're with Dom, finishing up everything before our move." Alice said as they ordered their drinks and took a table by one of the front windows. "So, you're going to move." Taby seemed so dejected that Alice didn't know what to say.

"Taby ..." She thought that they had already talked about this. Why was Taby so sad now?

"I know, babe. Dom's going. And really, I'm so happy for you; if anyone deserves this, it's you. A man that loves you, and a fresh start. I'll just miss you."

"You could come. Dominic would help you." Taby shook her head.

187

"Troy just got settled …"

"You know that's a cop-out, right? I know that it's a lot to ask, but it would be a fresh start for you, too." Her words were more heated than she wanted them to be, but she was frustrated. Taby was her best friend and she wanted her to come with them.

"Troy says that he won't ever leave." Taby's voice was sad and resigned, something altogether not very Taby-like.

"Is everything okay?" Alice asked, concerned.

"Yes. Of course. We just have a difference in how …" She paused and seemed to collect herself. "It doesn't matter. New topic?" she questioned. They talked for a while longer about Taby finishing school and coming to visit at Christmas. Alice was glad to see the dark cloud gone from over her friend's head.

They started to get up to leave, when there was a popping sound. It was an odd sound that she couldn't place, but she didn't have the time to process it as the front window shattered. Glass reining through the air to litter the floor around them.

It took a second for Alice to figure out what was happening. Looking around, she saw people frantically trying to get toward the back of the shop, shouting, screaming. Taby flung herself under the table where they had been sitting. She could hear yelling, and her brain finally kicked into gear as she dove after Taby at the same time that her guards reached them, covering them with their bodies. Alice's ears were ringing from the gunshots as glass from the windows rained down on them, dusting the floors around them.

"Get us out of here!" Randy, one of her guards, yelled toward the rest of the men. The other men were looking around but couldn't see anything from having to crouch down behind the small table they were using as shelter. Randy risked a peek up over the table, his head just barely over enough to see.

"The back door. It's our only chance." He was yelling but was still crouched, partially covering a terrified Taby. Another guard was covering her. She didn't even know who, the panic of the situation getting to her. Alice looked up as much as she could, glancing in his direction, about to ask him if they should call 911.

Randy's body jerked. She watched, horrified, as he slowly slid down toward the floor, not moving, a red spot right in the middle of his forehead. Dead.

He was dead.

Dead.

His empty eyes, open.

Dead.

Her brain scattered at the thought, that man had died trying to protect them.

"FUCK!" the guard closest to her yelled out, pushing her closer toward the floor, startling her out of her shock. *Not now,* she thought. Later she could freak out.

Just then she heard sirens, and men yelling and then the screeching of tires.

Then it was quiet.

Nothing but the sounds of the sobbing of the patrons in the restaurant.

"Come on. NOW!" The guard with her stood and took off, dragging her after him. His head swiveled back and forth, searching for any danger. She managed to snag Taby's hand right before she was swept up, dragging her with her.

Alice looked behind her, seeing that the two other men were on the floor; shot as well, but moving. She said a silent prayer for them, as they ran through the back door toward an alleyway and down the street. Alice could hear Taby crying behind her, but she didn't have much strength left.

All she knew was that she couldn't let go of the guard or Taby. That was what she focused on. Just not letting go.

"Get me an evac now! I'm in the alley behind Broadway and 3rd. Track my phone. I've got to get them out of here. I don't think so. No!" He was yelling into his phone.

Probably to Danny, she thought.

"Are we being followed?" Taby gasped out. Alice hadn't thought of that before.

"Not waiting around to find out. Move, now!" The guard's answer was short.

Alice bit back a sob, thinking of the man who had just died trying to save them. All she could hope for now was that Dominic would come for her.

They ran down an endless number of roads, twisting and turning. She was quickly becoming too tired to keep going, having to drag Taby behind her.

Just don't let go, she thought.

They rounded another corner and the guard in front of them paused. He was breathing just as hard as them as he looked over his shoulder and gestured them forward.

"Come on." Although she was just about done in for, she had a picture of Dominic in her mind. She knew that she had to keep going. For him. She could not do that to him.

She wouldn't leave him.

Just don't let go, she thought again.

She pushed with all her strength and followed the man in front of her. He was risking everything for her, and she didn't even know his name.

Chapter 30

Dominic was frantic.

Actually, at this point he was beyond frantic. Nobody knew anything, and he had been on the other side of town when everything went down.

Went down. Those were Danny's words.

"Fuck. How much longer!" he shouted, not caring who answered him, just wanting to know that she was all right. He could see her beautiful face from last night, lying in his bed with her hair fanned out around her. Love in her eyes directed at him. God, it was all for him, and he might lose that.

No, he couldn't think like that.

"Sir, we got a lock on his signal."

"Follow it!" Dominic shouted. They knew that James, the only guard left, had fled with Alice, contacting them soon after. So, they knew right where to go. He just prayed that when he got there, she was okay.

They came screeching to a halt in front of an alleyway that the SUVs couldn't fit through.

"Where is she? Where is she?" he yelled, his eyes frantically searching for any sign of her, them, *anything*. The side door was flung open to reveal a worried-looking Rick.

"Down the alley!" Thrusting a bullet proof vest at Dominic, Rick added, "Because I know you won't stay here." Rick started down the alley, leaving him to follow.

"Fuck!" He pulled on his vest while he and his men started down the alley.

"We have ten minutes, and we need to move out, I think everything is being tracked!" Danny yelled out from behind them, and Dominic resisted the urge to reach out and punch him for even suggesting they leave without finding her.

He would never leave her, *ever*.

They came down the alley and turned, only to be confronted by a man with a gun.

"Whoa!"

"Stop right there!"

"NO NO NO NO!"

They were all yelling at each other, including the man that they ran in to. His face was bloody, and he was holding his side and was tilted as if in pain. His face was familiar, though as Dominic tried to fight through his worry for Alice and concentrate on the moment at hand.

"Jason!" He stepped forward, but both Danny and Rick reached out to stop him.

"Jason, look at me!" Jason finally concentrated on Dominic, blinking he eyes like he was seeing him for the first time.

"Hey man, it's okay. You're okay now. We're here. You did good man. Okay." He stepped a little more forward and gestured for him to lower his gun. He looked slightly behind Jason and saw a large dumpster and knew that was probably where the girls were hiding.

Hope sailed through him that they might have made it in time.

"It's all good, man. Hey, listen, can you lower your gun? My girl, you got her out, right? Can I go to her?" He was trying to keep his voice calm even though he was raging at not being able to see Alice. Not knowing if she was okay. At the sound of Dominic talking about Alice, the man looked frantic.

"Shit! Taby!" Jason turned toward the dumpster, but before he could go any farther, he collapsed. Everyone ran forward, including Dominic.

Everyone went for Jason.

Dominic went for the dumpster.

"Behind the dumpster. I tried. I'm sorry," Dominic heard Jason say as he rounded the corner of the dumpster, sliding on the pavement, only to stop in horrified shock. Taby was lying on the ground, blood surrounding her in a hideous red circle.

Alice was nowhere to be found.

"Taby! God!" Dominic rushed, forward falling to his knees. His hand went to her face, gently patting.

"Taby come on. Wake up. I need to know where Alice is!" Her eyes fluttered open and she stared at him in blank silence. He shrugged off his jacket, pressing it into her stomach to where even he could see the huge gaping hole.

"Taby, where is Alice?" His hand on her cheek kept gently patting, trying to keep her awake. He knew she didn't have long. Knew it should bother him and that it probably would later. But right now, he wanted Alice. That was all that mattered.

"Took … Took-k-k-k," she stuttered out, blood dripping out of her mouth.

"Took what, who took? Alice? Did they take her?"

"Y… e … s."

"Call 911! Taby, hang on, help's coming."

"Tell T-T …" He couldn't make out her words but guessed that she was talking about Troy.

God! Troy!

She gasped, choking on her blood, reaching for his hand. Her grip was slight, and he worried that she wasn't going to hang on much longer.

"Yes. I will, but please, sweetheart, just hang on. You tell him yourself, okay?" He squeezed her hand. He ran his hand over her head and used his sleeve to wipe at the blood dribbling out of her mouth, the truth of the situation finally dawning on him.

"You tell him yourself. Please hang on."

He felt her hand go slack first. Then he watched as her chest slowly stuttered and her eyes fell closed.

"Taby, baby. No. Come on." Her hand slipped from his grasp as her body went slack.

"Call 911!" he yelled out again.

"Already did." Rick's solemn voice came from somewhere behind him, letting him know that they weren't alone.

"Taby!" he called to her again, but she was already gone.

And so was Alice.

You have to get out of here, Alice thought.

She knew that the longer she sat here, the worse her chances were of ever getting out. She still had no idea who was behind this, but she had a sneaking suspicion that Geo was involved.

Everything was because of him.

Her thoughts kept going back to the guard and Taby, hoping they were okay. They had thought that they were home free, and Jason had decided that hiding and waiting till Dominic could get to them was the best approach. It was all fine. Hiding behind a dumpster.

Then it wasn't.

A group of men had shown up. They had shot Jason in the side and had held a gun to his head. She'd had no choice but to come out of hiding, no matter how much Jason had been yelling at her not to. She wasn't going to watch another man die for her.

Taking one last look at Taby, she had stepped out. She should have known that Taby wouldn't just stay there. She stumbled out after her yelling,

"No! No! You can't! Alice!"

From there everything erupted. Bullets were flying and she was dragged away. She tried looking back to see if they were okay, but all she could see was Jason dragging Taby away.

God, she hoped they made it.

They had shoved her into a car, putting her in the middle with no access to get out. A guard sat on either side of her. As they were driving out, she had seen a cop directing them out of the traffic. He had been yelling at them that they had to get out before everybody else got there. Right then she knew that she was in bigger trouble than she thought. If the police were in on it, did she really even stand a chance?

As they drove in silence, she tried to keep track of all the turns. But eventually she lost track. They weren't taking the direct route, seeming to turn down every back road they came across. She was thinking that they were north of the city but wasn't sure when they turned in to a big farmhouse driveway.

A glimpse out the window confirmed her fear. They were way out in the middle of nowhere. Fields as far as she could see.

That brought her too now. In a cold, dark basement curled up in a ball, trying to figure out how to get out. She could almost scoff at the predictability of it. But she didn't. She needed every ounce of strength and wits about her to figure out how to get away. She wasn't going to just give up. No matter what they wanted or what they were going to do to her.

She wouldn't do that to Dominic. She wouldn't do that to her parents. And she certainly wasn't going to do that to herself.

She thought of Dominic and how much she loved him. How contradicting he was. So hard and commanding, yet caring and gentle with her. She hoped that they got a chance to build a life together. To have a family and kids. To see where their future took them. She thought of Danny and Rick, friends that she wouldn't trade for anything in the world. They had become her biggest champions. Making herself better at seeing what was given to her. They were always there to cheer her up.

Then Taby. Her best friend. The one who helped to teach her that there was more to life than her parents' wishes. That she could have a life, family, and friends. That she could have love. She hoped that she made it out okay. That she and Troy could build the life they so desperately wanted. It hadn't been easy for them, their past decisions haunting them. She hoped that they got the beginning that they needed so badly.

The memories of the friends and family that she had surrounded herself with gave her strength. She took a deep breath, letting their memories linger just a little longer. She would do this for them.

Looking around, she knew that she only had a small window of time to get this done. They hadn't tied her up, too content in believing that she was helpless. She knew that if they caught her, she wouldn't have a second chance; her only hope was the element of surprise.

There was a window along the far wall. She stood up slowly and carefully, not making any noise as she crept to the window. A glimpse outside showed that she was slightly above ground level, making it easy to get out. *She could do this*, she thought. There were fields and not many trees, but she didn't have any choice. If she could get out, then she could run.

It was a chance. A slim one. But she only needed one.

Hearing footsteps down the hall, she quickly crawled back to the corner and drew her knees up. She knew that she had to keep up the act. She heard the door creak open and heavy boots stomp across the floor toward her. She nearly passed out from fright but kept still, curled up in a ball, acting as if she was asleep.

After what felt like an eternity the man turned and walked out, shutting the door behind him. She waited for a second more to see if he was going to come back, but the sound of his feet was fading. She jumped to the window and tried to jimmy it, but it wouldn't budge. She saw a lamp sitting on the bedside table and an idea came to her.

Quietly as she could, she scooted the table in front of the door. It would not buy her a lot of time, but every second counted. She grabbed the lamp and, taking the shade off she hefted it in her hands, testing its weight. It wasn't super strong, but neither was the window. She figured that if she hit it hard enough one swing would work. She hoped anyway. Taking a deep breath, she swung with everything she had.

The noise was loud.

Very loud.

The men in the house had to have heard her, but she didn't stay around to find out. Hoisting herself up, she swung her legs over and jumped out the window. She felt the glass cutting her hands but didn't stop to look. The minute her feet touched the ground she took off. The sound of the men pounding on the bedroom door quickly faded as she took off at a diagonal across the field. If she could make it far enough there was a field of corn, there. She could use that to hide.

She ran like she hadn't ever run before, determined not to give up. Even once she hit the cornfield she didn't stop. Every once in a while, she would think that she heard something, but she didn't stop. Putting everything she had into her legs, she pumped them as fast as she could. Corn flew by her, whipping her in the face, arms, and legs. But she didn't stop.

Finally, lungs bursting, she emerged out of the cornfield onto a highway. There weren't a ton of cars but enough that there were people. She ran along the road, waving her arms, screaming for someone to stop. She didn't have a lot of time before those men would catch up to her.

It was pure luck that she even found the small highway. She didn't know how long she had run, but it had worked. If she could get a ride into a town, she could call Dominic. He would come to get her. She wasn't raised a religious person, but she knew that someone was looking out for her, because just a second after she made it to the road a car slowed down and stopped next to her.

"You all right, dear?" There were two older ladies in the car, looking like they were on their way to church. She knew it was stupid to get in the car of a stranger, but she didn't have a choice. Right now, she wasn't going to second-guess her luck. She would take the chance.

"No. Please, I'm being chased. I need to get to town to a phone so I can call for help." They looked quickly at each other then told her to climb in the back.

"We will get you to town, dear."

She felt her first wave of relief burst through her, bringing a wave of tears as the car pulled away and took off.

"Thank you," she managed to stutter out. Now that she wasn't running, the adrenaline was starting to wear off and the shakes were setting in. She just needed to hold on a little longer. She had to get to her Dom. Then everything would be okay.

"That's just fine, dear. We can take you right to the police station." Then she turned around in her seat to look at Alice.

"Are you okay, honey?" Alice was sure that she wasn't looking great, but she nodded anyway.

"Do you have a cell phone? I need to call someone," Alice asked. Not only did she know that Dom was going to be panicked, but she wouldn't feel truly safe till she was with him.

"Oh yes, honey, here." The lady handed back what looked to be an ancient flip phone. If it weren't for the situation, she would have laughed. She quickly dialed Dom's number, thankful that she knew it.

"Who is this?" The sound of his voice sent a fresh wave of tears through her, halting any response that she would have had. She felt dizzy with relief.

"God fucking damnit! I don't fucking have time for this! Who is this?"

"Dom?" she croaked out through her tears.

"ALICE! God, baby! Where are you? Are you okay? What happened? Where are you?" He burst out with too many questions to answer, and a laughing sob escaped through her tears.

"I'm okay. I got out." The whole story came pouring out of her, and she forgot the woman in front of her. She was so relieved to have him on the phone, nothing else mattered in that moment.

"Sweetheart, what road are you on? What town are they taking you to?" His voice sounded just as desperate as hers.

"Umm …" She held the phone away from her face slightly and addressed the woman up front.

"Where exactly are we headed?"

"We will be in Newfield in about fifteen minutes. There's a police station there."

"Dominic, did you hear that?" Her voice was cracking, barely able to talk.

"Yeah I did, baby. We'll be there before you. We're already on our way. Listen to me, okay? This is important."

"Okay." She glanced to the front then hunched back into her own seat, not knowing if it was safe for them to overhear. "What?"

"Do *not* go to the police. Okay? A lot has gone down, but I think this is a Familia problem. You are not safe with the cops right now."

She thought of the cop guiding them out of the area when she was taken.

"Dom," she whispered into the phone, "there was a cop there. He got the men who kidnapped me out."

"Fuck! Please baby, I'm coming. I'll get you out of this. I'm calling my father in, and Danny says we'll be in town next to the fountain. Go there, okay?"

"I will. Dom?"

"Yeah, sweetheart?"

"I love you." His groan was his answer.

"Fuck, baby. Please just get there. I love you too." Then the line went dead.

"Sounds like quite the bit of trouble you got yourself in." Obviously, the woman had heard more than she thought.

"Yes. But it's okay. Dominic, my … boyfriend." That word sounded weird to her. "My man, he's coming. He should be there before us. He said to meet at the fountain downtown."

"I'm guessing you have your reasons for not going to the police. Even if I don't agree. I have lived in this town my whole life. Those boys in the sheriff's station wouldn't do something like that." The woman sounded miffed that they weren't trusting the police. She just hoped that she didn't make too much of an issue.

"I'm sure they wouldn't, but we can't take that chance. It's safer for everyone if you can just drop me off and be on your way. I don't want to cause you any trouble."

"All right, dear." The lady didn't seem like she agreed to it at all, but all three of them drew silent after that. All Alice could do was wait.

Chapter 32

She could tell that they were coming to the outskirts of the town, and her nerves started to get the best of her, her hands clenching in her lap. When she saw the top of the fountain come into view she nearly jumped out of the car.

"Almost there, dear," the woman who was driving said, pulling in closer toward where the fountain was. She frantically searched for him, and the minute she found him she felt her heart flutter. He was standing in the middle of the square with Rick and Danny. The car had barely come to a stop before she was barreling out, crying out for him.

"Dom!" His head snapped toward her and he started running.

"Alice!" She flew into his arms, where he wrapped her uptight till she couldn't breathe. But she didn't care—he was here and that's all she wanted. She was sobbing, nearly incoherent, her arms wrapped around him, clinging for all that she was worth.

"Thank God!" he was chanting over and over. His hands were in her hair, wrapping around her. Pulling her in closer, his movements frantic.

"We need to move out now!" Rick was behind them, surveying the area.

"Are you sure you're okay, dear?" The lady who had picked her up asked, looking at them with a worried eye.

"Ma'am, I cannot thank you enough for helping her. She is everything to me. Just ..." Dominic paused and drew her in even closer. Her head was tucked under his chin, her arms wrapped around his strong back, and she never wanted to let go.

She heard his voice break as he told them, "Just thank you."

The lady dried her eyes with a hanky and simply nodded. Rick and Danny came up and, one on either side of them, ushered them toward the car as Dominic picked her up, cradling her in his arms, not letting her walk. She didn't mind. She would stay right where she was forever if she could.

She looked over Dominic's shoulder and saw the two ladies watching. Alice raised her hand in a farewell and mouthed 'thank you'. They nodded and waved back. She didn't know their names or who they were, but she would forever be grateful for them saving her.

Dominic climbed into one of the SUVs, all his men following, and they took off.

He pulled her closer to him. Her body was shaking, the adrenaline getting the best of her. She tried to steady her breathing, soaking up the feeling of being safe in his arms as they drove away.

***

Alice woke up laying on Dom's lap, listening to the gentle talk of the men around her. She was in a bed, so she figured that she must have fallen asleep on the drive here. She sat up and looked around, realizing it was a bedroom that she had never been in before.

"You don't have to do that. I know you have a life here, guys."

"We've already talked it over. It's a settled, man. There are a few other guys who are interested in following also. Maybe you could get them security jobs or something."

"Dom," she whispered as she got up and walked to the slightly open doorway.

"Hey, sweetheart." He gently rubbed her hair away from her face. "You okay? The doctor will be here soon." His concern touched her, but she didn't want to see any more people right now. She just wanted to stay right here in his arms. Some of the men who had been in the room left, leaving Danny and Rick with her and Dominic.

"I don't need one. I'm okay." She sat up on the bed and looked around. "Where are we?"

"For my piece of mind, okay?" he urged, ignoring her question, and all she could do was nod. Her head felt fuzzy and out of it. She knew that it was the adrenaline crash that was still affecting her.

"How is Jason? Is he okay? And Taby? Where is she?" Dom looked sideways toward Danny and Rick, and Rick quickly shook his head.

"What's going on?" When nobody answered her and Dominic wouldn't meet her eyes, she started to get a bad feeling.

"Dom, where is Taby?" A sinking feeling was starting in her stomach, spreading all through her. And before Dom even looked up at her she knew what he was going to say.

"NO … NO NO NO NO! She's okay, please tell me she's okay!" Her screaming was shrill, not wanting to comprehend what he was trying to tell her. She looked to Danny and Rick, knowing that they would tell her that this was all a really bad joke, but they just shook their heads.

"Dom, *NO!*" She started to shake. This couldn't be happening! Not Taby! She had to be okay!

"I'm sorry." There were tears in his eyes and she lost it.

She started screaming as he wrapped his arms around her, holding her as she pounded her hands on his chest.

"NOOOOOO!" Taby, her beautiful friend, couldn't be gone. She *couldn't*!

"I'm so sorry. So sorry. There wasn't anything else I could do. I'm so sorry," he kept whispering through her sobbing, but it didn't matter. Nothing mattered. Taby was gone and it was all her fault.

Chapter 03

"This should help her sleep."

The doctor finished and started packing up his stuff. Dominic continued to hold her in his arms, both of them propped up on pillows on the bed. She had screamed so long and hard, thrashing with a strength that he had never seen, till the doctor had to give her a shot to calm her down.

"Thank you," Dom murmured. His whole world was slowly falling apart, and he didn't know how to make it better. How was he supposed to help her with this? And what was he going to tell Troy?

God, Troy was probably frantic. Dominic had never even called him!

"You don't need to thank me. Your father and I were good friends for many years. I was happy to see him finally get to live his life. You can call me, but physically she will be okay." Dom just nodded and went back to watching her as the doctor left.

He had called his father after the ambulance showed up to take away Taby, and although he couldn't get here for another day or two, he sent Dominic some more men and gave him directions to a safe house out of state. He knew that he could handle this on his own but having his father here to look for Geo would allow him to focus on Alice's safety.

They were now two states away and would probably never be going back. He knew the city didn't hold any good memories for him any longer, and for Alice it would probably be even worse. He reached out and grabbed her hand, smoothing his hand over her soft skin.

"Dom." Rick was at the door, holding a phone.

"Troy," Rick told him quietly, and dread went through him at what he needed to do. Not wanting to show any weakness even now, he somehow found the strength to stand. Gently tucking the blankets around Alice, he took the phone, walking into the hallway.

He didn't want to know what this was going to do to Troy. He knew what he would be like if it was Alice who hadn't made it. She almost hadn't, and he still couldn't get the pressure off his chest. It was slowly crushing him, the frantic despair that he wouldn't be able to find her still sitting with him.

The weight of the task ahead of him overwhelming, he raised the phone to his ear. Taking a deep breath, he said a silent prayer that he was strong enough to do this. Rick stood there, Danny at his back like always, there to support him as he told one of his oldest and best friends that his girl was dead.

"Troy." He could hear the heaving breaths on the other end. Almost sobbing, and he knew that the man already knew.

"I'm so sorry, man. We don't know what happened. I got there too late." He trailed off, not knowing how to make it better. There were no words that would take away this pain.

"She's okay." Troy's voice was tortured.

"What?" Dom was puzzled. Was he in denial? Maybe asking about Alice?

"She made it through surgery. Flatlined three times. Not out of the woods, but she's made it," Troy said.

Relief flew through him, so strong his knees felt weak. He leaned against the wall, his strength almost failing him. Rick came to his side, holding his shoulder. Dominic allowed the comfort he needed now when the overwhelming relief was almost too much to take. He looked up and saw a smile on his friends' faces, knowing that they had heard the good news, too.

"Where are you guys? What do you need?" He immediately wanted to help.

"Your father called. He's getting us out of here. A safehouse."

"Alice will be glad to know that you guys are safe."

"She thinks Taby is gone?" Troy now just sounded tired.

"Yeah. We all did."

"I'm guessing you know the drill, or at any rate your father will be calling you soon, but we are going underground. With Taby like this, we can't be a part of this, man." He understood completely. If he could just take Alice and disappear, he would in a heartbeat.

"I understand. I'll miss you, man, but you take care of your girl."

"You as well. And tell Alice not to blame herself; I know she will."

"You take care, Troy." He could hear the man take a deep breath.

"Hey, Dominic?" His voice was stronger now.

211

"Yeah, man?"

"Maybe I'll take you up on that offer someday." Then the line clicked, and he was gone.

Sadness washed through him at what his longtime friend was going through; he could only pray that they would be safe. His father would take care of that. When it was safe, they could reconnect. But for now, this was best. To distance themselves from Alice and himself. He didn't know how deep the well of deceit went, and anyone attached to them wasn't safe.

Anger filled him at the thought that there was a definite leak of information within his ranks. His tired mind tried to find the lost pieces to the puzzle, but he couldn't quite put them together. His mind was foggy after being up for over twenty-four hours. The adrenaline and fear crashing made him even more tired.

"Alice will be glad to know," Rick said.

"Yeah." Dom was exhausted. He could feel the tiredness and stress slowly leaving his body a boneless mess.

"Hey, man. Get on in bed with your girl, okay? We've got this. You need to sleep to be any good for her."

Dominic, in a moment of weakness, let both Danny and Rick help him up and over to where Alice was sleeping. He lay down and pulled her into him, relishing the fact that she was in his arms once again. Then he followed her into sleep.

Chapter 34

Those next few days they stayed at the safehouse. Alice was glad that for a little time she didn't need to worry about anything. Her mind was shot with all the activity.

She had woken up and learned that Taby wasn't dead. That she had made it through surgery, but her relief was short-lived.

Learning the truth of just how bad the situation really was.

Both Taby and Troy were going to ground. She wouldn't get to say goodbye to her friend. They might never know the full extent of everything, and she never wanted to put her friend in that kind of danger again. So, she understood, but it was still hard. Knowing that she wouldn't get to talk to her, to tell her how sorry she was that she had been dragged into this whole mess.

Dominic was right there by her side. Stronger than ever. There to be anything she needed. She knew that he wasn't having a much better time mourning his friendship, with Troy, but he didn't let it show. Only with her, late at night when it was just the two of them curled around each other, would he let down his walls. His fear over the future getting the best of him as he fucked into her over and over. His movements grasping and frantic, both in love and panic. It was desperate.

It was everything they both needed.

They both had hope that someday they would see their friends again. That their lives could go back to normal, but it wasn't something that was likely to happen any time soon.

Dominic's father Sergio had gone straight to the city. He was going deep into the world that both men had worked so hard to leave in search of Geo. She knew that it ate at Dominic to not be able to find Geo himself. But when she asked him about it, he said that his job right now was her safety.

They were both exhausted. The last days of turmoil had taken their toll on both of them. But Dominic never wavered. While she let her mind and body recover from everything, he was deep in planning with his men. Going over plans, commanding as ever. Never letting anything skip by them.

While Dominic was busy doing all that, he'd had everything from their home moved to their new place. The one they were supposed to be moving to in a couple of weeks. It would be there when they were ready to move on. Their plan of a future was still there, they just had to wait till the coast was clear.

Yesterday several of Dominic's men had left. It had been emotional to see him say goodbye to men he had worked with and grown up with, but with Dominic leaving the area and not part of Familia anymore they had no option but to go. Ivanov had pulled out. Determining that he wasn't a part of it, he had said that he wouldn't help them anymore. He wouldn't stop them from searching for Geo and anything else that they needed to do. But he also wouldn't help them. She guessed that was the best that they could hope for at this point.

"I owe you guys more than you will ever know. If there is ever anything that I can do for you. I wish you all the best," Dominic had told his men.

Six of his men had left. However, she was just as surprised and happy to find that four had decided to stay along with Danny and Rick. They told her that they were due for a fresh change. It was nice to know that they would have friends with them when this was all over. Although she didn't know some of them very well, she was looking forward to them being a part of their fresh start.

Today they were moving to another safehouse farther east. They were still playing it safe for a while till they had a better handle on just who the players were and what was going on. Dominic felt that it was best until they were able to find Geo.

"Hey sweetheart, you just about ready?" Dom came in, carrying the last of their stuff from the bedroom. She nodded.

"What's up? You okay?" He came up to her and cupped her cheek, sliding his other hand toward the back of her neck. He was getting good at reading her emotions, and she knew that he would just keep pushing till she told him.

"I just wish I could have said goodbye." He knew who she was talking about. He had been her rock to lean against as she had worked through her emotions about everything. As she tried to not break down crying again, he wrapped her in his arms, holding her tight.

"I know, but they're safe. That's what matters, baby." She nodded, knowing that having her friends safe was worth more than having them with her.

"It's okay to miss her." She loved his support. He knew just what she needed. He kissed her forehead and stepped back.

"Come on. Let's head out. Maybe we can find a decent coffee shop for Your Highness." She chuckled and swatted at his arm. His teasing helped to lighten the mood.

"It's not my fault that you guys make terrible coffee."

"I do not make bad coffee," Rick said indignantly, coming into the room, making her laugh at him. Rick was very territorial about his cooking skills, coffee included. The problem was that he really *was* terrible at it.

They all climbed into two vehicles, Danny was in the SUV behind them, while Dominic Rick, Alice, and a guard whose named she had learned that morning was Jack, were in the front SUV.

Both vehicles drove carefully down the little dirt drive that led to the house. It was located deep in the forest in the mountains. The driveway was barely wide enough for their vehicle to fit and it helped to discourage anyone driving by it. Not that there would be that many. They were a good hour and a half from any town. How Dominic's family came to own this house she didn't know, but right now she was grateful for the reprieve that it had given them.

"What's that?" This came from Rick in the front as he slowed the vehicle. Both Dominic and she leaned forward toward the front, looking out at the gate where a piece of paper was stuck to it.

"Was that there this morning?" Dominic questioned, using the mic attached to his ear like all the guards had.

"No—there wasn't anything out of the ordinary, sir." This was called from another guard in the vehicle behind them, over the coms. She really was going to have to get everybody's names straight.

"Jack, you want to check it out." Rick gestured to the guard in the passenger seat.

"Yes, Sir," and she watched as he stepped out of the vehicle. He walked slowly toward the gate, head twisting as if looking for something. When he got to the gate, he seemed to lean down to read it, and after a second he snatched it up and jogged back toward them, his head still swiveling back and forth.

"Sir," he addressed, climbing in and handing the note over to Rick, who read it out loud.

> "He's out to get you. You have to go. I'm so sorry for everything. I didn't know. I'm sorry."-M

"It's signed with an M," Rick finished.

Everyone was quiet for a while.

"M, for Melissa?" Alice questioned. That was the only thing that made sense. But why would she be warning them?

"Why would she warn us?" She turned to Dominic. He didn't look at her and instead was focusing on the letter. His scowl deepened when he suddenly bit off a quiet,

"Rick."

"I know. Fuck!" Rick flipped his phone open and started barking out orders to whoever was on the other end.

"We're getting out of here," Rick said, looking over his shoulder to Dominic.

"Is everything okay?" she asked. Dominic sat back with her in the seat and wrapped his arm around her. His body was strung tight as he drew her closer to him, turning his head to kiss her forehead. He leaned down and whispered quietly, for only her to hear.

"No one should have known where we are, but it's okay. We will figure it out."

He was trying to reassure her, but she could tell that he was nervous. His body was tight and a frown was on his face. She laid her head on his shoulder and listened to everything around her. Dominic was talking to his father and Rick was talking to Danny in the other car. There was so much going on that her head was swimming again, the last few days of respite disappearing quickly.

Why was Geo doing this? Why couldn't anyone find him? She felt a deep wave of exhaustion sweep over her, even though it was still early in the day.

Taby getting shot, guards dying, all the upheaval. All because this one man wanted something. She just didn't understand what he wanted.

"Thanks. Yes, sir. Okay." Dominic got off the phone, looking even more worried.

"Melissa's body was found in a parking garage downtown." Alice gasped, and several profanities were muttered.

"Dad had Jason moved to a different hospital just as a precaution. I'm still not sure how they found this safehouse, though. Nobody should have known." Dominic was scowling out the window.

"Bet he's pissed." Rick chuckled darkly while driving. She watched as his hands clenched the steering wheel. A rare tell of emotion from him.

"Why?" Alice asked, puzzled.

"Because that means that more than likely someone gave up the information. Someone on his team." Rick's tone was sinister, but not as evil as the voice that spoke next. Shocking all of them in the car. Fear slid down her spine.

"Or yours," Jack stated from the front passenger seat at the same time that Rick's back went straight, and the guard whipped out a gun. Pointing it at Rick.

"Fuck," Dominic started with a dark tone to his voice.

Cold and unforgiving.

He wasn't just mad, he was livid. She could feel it wrap around them even as she leaned further into him, knowing that he would keep her safe. He placed his arm over her as if trying to shield her from the madman in front to them.

She gasped as Jack waved the gun at Rick. "Drive."

"What do you want?" Dominic asked in a cold voice.

"I want Rick here to drive. And you need to shut up." His voice was different and had a slight accent to it that she hadn't ever noticed before. Was he really hiding with them the whole time?

"Where am I headed?" Rick clipped out.

"Just head south. I'll tell you where from there." Dominic reached over and grasped her wrist, squeezing slightly.

She knew he was trying to comfort her, but she was consumed with terror. The gun was so close, and although so little it looked scarier than anything she had ever seen.

"Fuck," Rick muttered again while glancing behind them in the mirror, and she watched Jack smirk cruelly at him.

Both she and Dominic glanced behind them to see the other SUV come to a slow stop, smoke coming from its hood. That meant there wasn't anyone coming to help.

Danny and the other men were left sitting on the side of the road as they drove away.

A tear leaked down her cheek as she watched Danny jump out of the vehicle, standing there watching them drive away.

Would she ever see him again?

Her future was being torn apart right before her eyes. Her friends were nearly killed and ripped apart. She turned her head into Dominic's shoulder and tried her hardest to get her emotions under control.

She needed to have everything in control if they were going to survive this.

Chapter 35

It wasn't long before they started seeing signs for the next town. And her anxiety grew. She didn't know what was going to happen, but she knew that it was probably going to be soon.

"Take the next exit. Park at the gas station."

Rick followed the instructions and pulled into the gas station along the side of the road. There was another vehicle there, and when they got close several men in suits got out. Dominic tensed even more, and she looked out the window worriedly. They were seriously outnumbered now. The men surrounded the vehicle, one of them shouting out orders.

"Get out. And don't try anything." With no other choice they all climbed out, Dominic keeping a tight hold of her hand and placing his body slightly in front of hers. The guard watched them and then suddenly smirked.

"You think that you can stop this." It was a statement. "That maybe if you stall long enough someone will help you. It isn't going to work. What my boss wants he always gets." Dominic's body was stone, his grip on her tightening, but he didn't answer.

Jack reached behind him and pulled out several sets of zip ties, tossing them at their feet.

"Tie him up, babe," he instructed her. She glanced sideways to see that Rick was already tied up and being held down by two men. She didn't know what to do other than exactly what he asked. She might not be able to save herself, but she could save Dominic and Rick.

"No," Dom stated instantly. Jacks smirk was downright sinister, and he fired a warning shot at the ground just inches from their feet. She screeched, jumping back in shock.

"Easy there, princess." He sneered again and Dominic drew her completely behind him.

"What do you want?" Dominic asked. She knew that if they used those ties nothing good was going to come of it. But what choice did they have?

"Nothing from you," he stated cryptically, gesturing to the ties again. "Now."

"No." Dom's voice was powerful and strong.

"You still didn't tell us what you want." It was Rick this time, asking from his position on the ground.

"Put. Them. On. Last chance."

She was shaking. She didn't know what they were going to do, but she knew that Dom wouldn't ever put them on. He wouldn't give up his control like that. She didn't think that Rick would either. She needed to think of something fast.

"Fine." The shot was loud, and she screamed again, but this time because she watched Rick fall backward to the ground. His bound hands held his shoulder as blood seeped through his fingers.

"Fuck!" Dominic's harsh shout echoed just as loud as the gunshot had. He moved to take a step back, keeping her behind him.

"Now. Put them on him, Alice; there's no one to save you. Do it!" Dominic looked around the gas station and then back at her. They were running out of time and couldn't stall any longer. Her heart broke as she slowly started to move away from him.

"I love you," she whispered to him.

She needed him to know without a doubt that she loved him and didn't regret anything. He had given her the greatest love that she could have ever hoped for. But her time was running out. She bent over and grabbed the zip ties. Slowly hoping with everything she had that it wasn't the last time that she would get to touch him, she put the zip ties on him. First his legs then his hands. She could feel him looking at her, his gaze searing. At last it was done, and she looked into his eyes one last time before turning to face whatever was to happen.

Jack stepped up, and she moved to the side so as not to be close to him. He checked her zip ties and tightened them even further. Dominic didn't move or flinch, not even when she could see that they were biting into his skin.

"Now that that's done, you're coming with me, princess." Two men came up and grabbed her, leading her away.

"No!" Dominic shouted. "It's me you want. Leave her out of it!" he yelled, wrestling with his bound hands.

"You?" Jack laughed as he walked back toward where a van was parked.

"Sorry, but it's not you he wants. It's her." She could see Dominic's face go white with the realization that he wasn't able to save her.

They had all thought that he was the target, that using her was a way to get to him! And now he was tied up and unable to help her. He started twisting and bucking, trying to get loose as she was dragged away. She started screaming, knowing that this was it.

"Shut the fuck up or I'll shoot him!" one of the men yelled out and she went silent, still fighting to get one last glimpse of her man.

He was shaking his head, twisting and pulling with everything he had. Trying to get to her. She knew that he would fight till the end to keep her safe and with him. But this was out of their hands. She didn't want to leave him, but she wouldn't let him be hurt.

Too many people had been hurt because of her. And she couldn't let Dominic be one of them. In that instant, she stopped fighting the guards hauling her away.

"Alice! Fuck!" She turned toward him one last time, studying his face, wanting to commit every part of him to memory.

"I love you," she mouthed, not knowing if he saw it or not, right before she was shoved into the vehicle. She looked over her shoulder one more time to see Dominic struggling for all he was worth. Rick was lying next to him on the ground, bleeding.

"I'll find you. You motherfucker! Alice!" he cursed out, not letting up on his hands and feet. She let the last vision of him and Rick there on the ground fill her up. Tied up, but safe.

"He will be just fine, princess. Boss wants him alive." The words were her only hope at the moment. That they would be safe. That's all that mattered.

She felt a pinprick in her neck and started to turn around, only she felt her world turn. Her body started to slide down toward the floor of the SUV, the world wavy and twisting around her. Right before she slid into the darkness she saw a flash of Dominic's beautiful face, smiling at her.

Then nothing.

***

"Alice!" Dom kept calling, long after he knew that she could hear him.

"FUCK!" He kept trying to wiggle out of his zip ties, but it wasn't fast enough for him. The bastard had twisted them extra tight. Finally getting one hand loose he reached over to Rick, who was going in and out of conscience.

"Come on man, wake up." Rick groaned. He blinked his eyes open slowly then looked around, confused.

"Alice, where's Alice?" Rick croaked, and then groaned again. Dominic didn't answer, too intent on getting his feet free.

"*Ahhh*!" He cried out with savage anger as the last tie snapped, leaving him free. It was just too late. She was gone. He quickly crawled over to Rick and started to work on his ties.

"Knife … pocket," Rick croaked. Dominic reached into his pocket and drew it out, cutting the last of the ties off of them.

"There, sit up. I have to go get our phones." He didn't waste a minute as he scrambled up and dashed to the car. Throwing open the door, he frantically searched till he found someone's phone. Then he dialed Danny.

"Pick up. Pick up …" he muttered.

"Where the hell are you guys? Why didn't you stop?" Danny shouted in greeting. He seemed just as frantic, but there wasn't time to explain. Those men had a head start and Dominic sure as fuck wasn't going to lose her.

Not this time.

Not again.

"Track this phone. We're at a gas station off the highway, southbound, exit 146. Jack was working for Geo. They got Alice."

"Fuck! Where's Rick? They got Alice?"

"Rick's been shot. Shoulder, through and through. They took Alice." Just saying the words sent a shard of pain through his heart. He let it fill him, though. The red-hot anger. The overwhelming fear for her. Let it all fill him up till he was consumed. He would use it. No one took what was his.

He had honestly thought that the man would leave her be. Shoot him, stab him, he didn't know and didn't care. As far as they knew she had only been drawn into it because of him. The mess with her uncle hadn't brought about anything. They hadn't been able to find a track that involved her. She was just there as a pawn to get to him. Geo was after him for revenge and the money that he had tried to steal.

Why the *fuck* would he want her?

"Man! Boss! Dominic!" He realized that Danny was shouting at him.

"They took her," he croaked out, feeling like he couldn't breathe.

Focus Dominic, he thought.

God! She had sacrificed herself for him. If there was ever a doubt that she loved him, that just proved it. She had put herself

226

in that sociopath's hands, and she had to have known what would happen.

"I'm only about five out, okay? Is Rick okay, man?" Dom looked over his shoulder at the man. He was breathing heavily but it looked like the bleeding had slowed down. He was watching Dominic, then slowly nodded his head. He knew that Danny would be asking about him.

"He says he's okay."

"Good, good." He could hear the relief in his voice. The two men were closer than brothers. Then, like a light bulb turning on, it came to him.

"Her bracelet," he growled out. "I need my fucking computer," he muttered as he ran to the back of the vehicle.

"Her chip!" Danny was talking to him and someone in the background, but he didn't care.

He had forgotten about the bracelet. Something that he had only just given her, wanting something like the watch that his men wore. He had been grateful at the time that she hadn't pitched a fit over the tracker, seeming to know that it was important to him.

Logging on to the site, he saw that Danny was indeed really close to them. Only about a minute out.

"I can see you. I've already called 911 for Rick," Danny said as Dominic searched through the list for her tracker. He clicked on her link and saw that there was one red dot that was moving.

Moving *fast*.

It was her.

"I've got her." Danny's SUV came screeching into the lot, the police hot on his tail. Danny flew out of the vehicle, nodding to him as he ran to Rick.

"We'll get her." The hand on his shoulder finally drew his eyes away from the screen to look at the man behind him, Mark.

He was one of the guards that had requested to move to Florida with him. He'd been with his father before and now he was here. Dominic knew that he could trust him.

"Let's go." He knew that it probably made him a bad person, but he didn't even stop to check on Rick. He grabbed the computer, running straight to the second SUV and climbing in.

The back door opened, and Dominic turned around to see Danny climbing in.

"Rick?" he questioned quickly, too consumed with thoughts of her to complete the sentence.

"He's good. The ambulance has him, he wants me to come. Now go!"

Dominic didn't wait another second. He took off. He would get her. No matter what. He wouldn't accept anything less. He just hoped that she could hold on that long.

Chapter 36

She could hear everything going on.

She had woken up with a hood over her head and in the back seat. She didn't know how long they had been driving, but from the light coming in through the window she guessed that it was still daytime. The hood over her head might have prevented her from seeing, but it didn't stop her from hearing everything. She tried to catalog it all so she could remember it later, because this time she wasn't going to go willingly.

Not that she ever really had. She knew now what her uncle was capable of. If Geo was only half of that, then she knew that she was in big trouble. She didn't know what he wanted her for. After all, it was Dominic who had all his money. It didn't matter now anyway.

She had been able to save Dominic and hopefully Rick. Danny wasn't far behind them and he would get them help. Then Dominic would come for her. She had no doubt. She just had to hang on long enough.

The car slowed and she heard the tires hitting gravel, knowing that they must have left the main road.

"We're here," the man next to her said.

His voice didn't sound familiar, but he held that same accent. It almost sounded Russian. But she didn't think that was right. Ivanov was the only Russian they knew, and he had stepped back. She knew that none of Dominic's men had it, and neither had Geo as far as she knew. She didn't know any names other than the man who had betrayed them, Jack. She wouldn't forget that name. Ever.

"Get out!" was called to her, and she tried to scoot toward what she thought was the door, but it wasn't easy. With the hood she couldn't see, and her hands were tied behind her back. She heard a big sigh then hands were on her, lifting her out.

"Don't have all day," was grumbled at her. Then, gripping her arm, he marched her forward.

She could hear more boots behind her and knew that the other men were following them. She heard a door creak and then they were walking into a room. It was warm and smelled stale but clean. Almost like a hotel.

"Ah, you found her."

That voice. The same accent as the other men. That voice, she knew it somehow. A chill went down her spine, as the hands on her forced her to sit, then yanked her hood off.

The bright lights momentarily blinded her, and she blinked several times to clear it away. Looking around she saw that they were indeed in a hotel. A simple one with one bed, a table and chair, and a sink outside the door to the bathroom.

"I apologize as the accommodations are less than standard as you can see, but I will change that soon enough. I was … impatient to get to you."

She looked at the man in front of her. Tall and older, maybe sixty or so, but he still looked to be in great shape. In a sharp business suit, he was nothing like what she had pictured a kidnapper to look like. He looked familiar but she couldn't place him.

The bigger question was what he wanted, she wondered.

"Do you remember me? You should." The man didn't seem put off by her non-remembrance, though, as she shook her head. Something about him seemed off. As if the air around him was poisoned, sending out trendles of evil through the air that she could feel crawling along her skin.

"The man you called 'uncle' worked for me. I was at your house a few times. I have to say, freedom looks better on you than the chains you used to wear." She flinched at the memory of what her uncle had done to her, but then she paused as his words started to sink in.

"I see that stumped you. You may ask me your questions." His voice was formal and courteous as he leaned back in his chair. A clear opposite of the situation that she was in.

"Why am I here?" she asked the most pressing question. He just stared at her, not answering her, his face never changing as he tilted his head, seeming to study her.

"Do you not know?" His question was said in a quizzical tone, but she felt as if it was a trap.

There was movement behind the man, and she looked up to see Geo standing by the window in the room, looking out over the parking lot below. Her eyes widened and she leaned back in her chair as if to escape, but there was no escape.

"I see you've met my grandson. A lot of trouble he has caused, I'm afraid. Too much attention is a very bad thing, you see." The man leaned forward.

"Where are my manners? My name is Igor Leonid. You may call me Leo. This name means something to you?" His slight accent was more pronounced when saying his name.

She still didn't know him, though. He sighed as if this whole situation was becoming an inconvenience to him. He unbuttoned his suit jacket and leaned back in his seat. She looked over to Geo who stood behind him, staring out the window blankly. Now that she was looking, she could see small resemblances between the two men. She wasn't sure who she was more afraid of, and her eyes kept going between the two men. Not knowing who she should be watching.

"Ignore Geo for now." She turned her eyes back to the man in front of her, Leonid. She needed to keep him occupied if she was going to find a way to get out of this.

"You said the man I called uncle? What did you mean?"

"Ahh, yes. Well, let me tell you a little story. There was a man once who was my rival. He was very good at what he did. He bested me in almost everything; he had no weakness, you see. Very hard to beat. One day I found out that he had hidden his family, that his sister had a little girl."

"My uncle?" she asked, terrified at where this conversation was going.

"Yes! Very good! Although not the man you knew. He was not really your uncle. I needed someone to impersonate the man that I killed. You understand, yes. It needed to be done." She shivered at the way he stated it, like she should be okay with it. Like it was something as easy as slicing bread, but she nodded anyway.

"The whole thing is an unfortunate circumstance. You were never meant to leave." He paused. "I was at your house only a couple of times, you see. I wanted you. So pretty with big eyes.

232

My prize. I take the man's land and pretty niece. So, I take you. You were meant to stay locked up. I may be a ... monster as people say. But my woman would be of age. Make a good wife that way. However, you were let go. I was never sure how that happened, by the way." She had to clear her throat to speak.

"He was drunk and forgot to chain me," she said.

It was the first time she saw true emotion cross the man's face. It was anger, and she knew that she never wanted that directed at her. She could feel the menace coming off him, but he seemed to get a hold of it a second later.

"No matter. The fucker is dead now." He waved it away with a flick of his wrist. His accent deeper as his anger lingered in his words.

"Did you kill him, too?" She whispered.

"Unfortunately, no. I did not get the chance. He died of a heart attack, if you didn't know. Stupid bastard loved his American fast food." He chuckled and shook his finger at her. "Very bad for you."

Geo shifted by the window and her gaze left Igor for the moment. Geo stayed in his position, never glancing at her, looking out the window with a blank expression. Her gaze came back to the man in front of her to see that he had been watching her, a sinister smirk on his face. Seeming to enjoy her terror at the situation.

"Yes, little pet, it was unfortunate that you had to meet up with my grandson." He gestured to Geo. "Lucky for me, though, or I would not have found you. I had been looking for a long time. It was very lucky for me that you came to meet Dominic. I might never have found you otherwise. You were good at hiding."

"I didn't think anyone was looking for me."

"Yes. Well, no matter. Geo was already in place for me, but so greedy. It is a family trait. His mother was such a greedy slut. He is here for his revenge. He is consumed with it. Such a mess." His hand waved in the air.

"You said the man who played my uncle worked for you?" She needed to keep him talking.

"Why yes. You see, I am the real head of the Western Crime Family." She felt her eyes go round in shock, mute for the moment. That wasn't what she was expecting, it was something that she knew not even Dominic knew. He smirked at her, seeming to like the reaction from her.

"It is okay. Not many know. I like it like that."

She tried not to flinch as he leaned forward, reaching out and grasping her chin, tilting her head as if she was a specimen for him to study. She tried to work up the courage to say something else, anything else, but her fear was starting to get the best of her. Everything that she and Dominic thought they knew was all a fake front to hide this man. She had to give him credit, though. She didn't think that even Sergio knew this.

"Sir," a man at the door stated. Igor dropped her chin, leaning back to look at the man. "There seems to be some incoming traffic."

Rage came over Igor's face and he turned to the man standing behind her.

"You searched her?"

"Sir?" The man's voice wavered, and he took a step back.

"Did you *FUCKING* search her!" he screamed, spittle flying out of his mouth. The guard behind her stuttered, his mouth flapping like a fish. He was deathly pale and shaking when he muttered a 'no'.

Before the man could even utter another sound, Igor drew his gun quicker than she could blink and shot him. She screamed, throwing her hands over her head as the guard dropped to the ground.

"Stupid fucker." He put his gun away and came over to her.

"Stand up." When she shrank away from, shaking, her terror getting the best of her and she whimpered, he reached forward and slapped her. The sound reverberated around the room as the force of it flung her sideways out of her chair, leaving her reeling on the floor.

With her hands tied behind her back she couldn't brace her fall and she fell painfully on her shoulder. Her head spun and throbbed. She distantly heard him tell her to stand up again, and she knew that she needed to, but she couldn't get her body to listen to her. Someone grasped her wrists from behind her, yanking her up, pulling her arms unnaturally, and she cried out.

"Look at me," Igor stated.

She looked up at him the best she could through the tears in her eyes, her face already starting to swell. She was so scared at that moment, but she knew one thing.

She would not give in.

She would fight.

For her.

For Dominic.

For them.

"Ahh, so fierce." He chuckled darkly and smoothed his fingers over her cheeks, and she had to fight the urge to gag. She wouldn't give him the satisfaction. "I like that in my woman, you know."

"Search her!" he commanded stepping back.

Two men from either side came at her. She instantly started fighting and screaming, kicking out the best she could before they got a hold of her. One had his arms wrapped around her arms from behind, the other was trying to get her feet, but she wasn't making it easy.

"Enough!" It was loud enough that she startled. Igor reached forward, griping her chin in a grip so forceful that she whimpered.

"You will let them search you. Am I understood? You do not want my wrath." She stared at him with hatred. His stare was frightening, no doubt, but she wasn't going to give in. She did, however, see the need to stall and to have the strength to fight and get away when she could. There were too many here, she couldn't do anything now. She would bide her time. When it was right, she would escape. So, for now she nodded her head in acceptance.

"Good girl." Those words sent a chill of disgust through her. Igor stepped back and gestured to the men to continue.

She stood rigid as they stripped her down to her bra and underwear. One grabbed her wrist and took the bracelet that Dominic had given her. She wanted to snatch it back to keep just a little piece of him with her but settled for a glare at Igor.

She looked at the back of the room to see Geo staring at her body, his eyes traveling from her feet to her chest till finally meeting her eyes. He grinned at her then turned and proceeded to stare out the window, as if he was watching for something.

Or *someone*.

"This must be it," one of the men said and handed the bracelet to Igor. He took it, turning it over in his hands. With a flick of his wrist, he let it fall, where he promptly smashed it with his foot. Her heart broke with it.

"We will leave now." Igor turned around and drew a shirt from a suitcase and handed it to her. "Put it on. From now on, nobody sees what's mine."

She nearly didn't take it, but she didn't want to be left standing in only her bra and underwear. Those words were so close to exactly what Dominic had said to her once upon a time. Then, it had given her a thrill of desire. Now, it sent a chill of fear through her. She couldn't stand there without anything on, though.

She grudgingly took it and slipped it on, buttoning it up. She could tell that it was his, not because it was huge on her but because it had his initials on the shirt pocket. She internally rolled her eyes at that vain gesture.

"Do you not like my shirt?" he asked, as if he had caught her look. She didn't say anything.

Don't piss him off, she thought.

He drew closer, and she stiffened when he wrapped his arm around her. The other arm came up to grasp her chin in a tight hold.

"Don't worry, my pet—you'll wear my brand soon enough." She flinched at his words, thinking that she would rather die, and he chuckled at her revulsion and ran his nose up the side of her face.

"Soon, pet." His words rang out in the small room.

Chapter 37

Don't panic.

Don't panic!

It didn't matter how many times he said the words in his head, he was panicking!

He knew that he needed to settle down and concentrate on the task at hand, but right at this moment all he could think about was that she was out there and not with him. Anything could be happening to her.

Hell, she could be dead, and he would be too late.

"Son, you need to calm down." His father's words didn't penetrate his frantic fear, but he nodded anyway. At this point, it wouldn't do to mouth off to the man since he was trying to help. He was slowly losing it, though.

After they left the gas station where he had lost her, Danny had the foresight to contact his father. Lucky for them, he had already been on the way to meet them and take them to their new safehouse. It meant that they now had more men, men who were watching him break down.

"I think it's probably a good thing I didn't go into the family business. I'm not cut out for this." His father chuckled beside him.

"You would think so but, alas, this would have made you better. A made man is never more dangerous than when he has something to protect. No matter, though. You would have done well no matter what you did. I raised a strong man."

"How far are we out?" Danny swung the computer his way and he studied the map. She seemed to have stopped. He didn't know if that was a good thing or a bad thing, but he was going to take it as a good one. Allowing them to make some headway on catching up to her.

"This exit," he told the driver.

His father, Danny, and he were in the SUV, while the rest of the men came in the other four vehicles behind them. A combination of his father's and his own men. He zoomed the computer screen in till he could see that her location was at a hotel.

"Take a left. It's the hotel on the left."

"Okay, men." His father reached under the seat and pulled out a case that held extra ammo and weapons. He handed him one of the handguns and an extra clip.

"Just in case." Dominic nodded back.

Because he knew that his father was thinking about his late wife, that this situation with Alice could end up being just like the one where Dominic lost his mother, he took the gun. He put it in the holster under his suit jacket, the other side holding his personal 9mm. His ankle holster was also strapped in place. He normally didn't carry more than one gun on him at a time,

His guards always followed him and there was never an issue. This was different. He needed every advantage he could get.

"There it is. Do you see those vehicles?" It was easy cause there weren't but three cars in the whole lot. Tinted and blacked-out large SUVs. Dominic would bet his last dollar they were armor-plated, too. They stood out like a sore thumb in a place like this. Definitely not one of the classier places.

"What room, guys?" a man called from the back seat and Dominic paused, thinking the man had a point. Now where did they start? Maybe Danny could hack their logs, although looking at the dump in front of him, he seriously doubted they even had a computer.

They didn't have to worry about it for long.

One of the doors on the lower level opened and five men stepped out, guns held high. As if in a horror movie he saw her. She was walking, being led in front of a man that Dom had never seen. She had on a man's shirt, and even though she was the most beautiful thing he had ever seen fury filled him when he saw that a man's shirt was all that she had on.

He knew that no matter what happened here, that the man holding her wasn't leaving alive. He started to leave the vehicle, but then paused. Watching as the last man stepped out of the hotel room.

Geo.

"Everybody file out. They cannot leave here. We will not get this chance again," he told the men, taking charge of the moment. Knowing that he wasn't leaving here without her. It wasn't an option.

He walked out in front of the car door, his father and Danny with him. The other men were behind them, taking up spots, ready should anything start to go down. Sergio spoke first as Dominic surveyed the area, trying to figure out how he was going to get her out of this alive.

"Ahh ... Igor. I knew that you would never be happy with that piss spot that your father gave you. Had to come take over in the States, did you?" his father said.

Dominic recognized the name but couldn't place the face. Igor Leonid was a big-time skin seller in the European Crime Family. He didn't have much territory. He wasn't much of anything really. A go-between man. Dominic didn't even know that he was in the States let alone here close to them.

"Let me guess, you're the face behind the West Coast Syndicate. The reason we cannot find answers," Sergio spoke out, answering Dominic's questions.

"Surprise! But you never did catch me. Nobody did! Not when it mattered," Igor said, shrugging.

He had a very arrogant air about him that set Dominic off. He had his arm wrapped around Alice, his hand in her hair. Dominic could tell that he was pulling hard, as she had her head tilted back so far. Enough that she could only look at Igor.

The bastard was doing it on purpose, he thought.

"Seems like I caught you at just the right time. Taking off with my son's woman."

The man laughed and Dom felt it along his nerves. He wanted to reach out, wrap his hands around his neck and squeeze. Every once in a while, Alice would give a tug against Igor's hold, but the man would only tighten his grasp.

Squeeze till his eyes bugged out of his motherfucking head, he thought.

Igor suddenly turned her around and said, "I'm afraid you must be mistaken. This is my pet." Igor's move placed Alice in front of him, shielding himself behind her body. It also gave himself a prime position, allowing the fucking bastard to run his nose along her neck.

The coward.

Dominic wasn't very close, but he could see a slight trembling in her body. Her bound hands were in front of her, twisting and pulling.

"Finders keepers, was it not?" Igor stated with a smirk over Alice's shoulder.

Dom would kill him for that smirk.

Nobody touched what was his.

"Not when you take it. You know that. So, what are we going to do?" His father was losing his patience. His voice had dropped an octave, a sure sign that he was starting to get pissed.

"The only option is for you and your pack of mutts to leave." Igor's voice betrayed his tension in the moment. But at the word 'mutts,' all the men behind him tensed. This man was really asking for it.

"You send in your men to rob my son, then you take his woman. You then have the balls to call my family a pack of mutts and expect me to walk away without the girl or any compensation? You really are a crazy Russian bastard." While the words coming out of Sergio's mouth were calm, Dominic knew better. So did Igor, by the tightening of his body and face. Sergio was not a man to piss off; if you did, you would *burn*.

"Compensation, huh?" Igor repeated, as if considering the words. Then looking around, he nodded once. Pulling out his gun he turned toward Geo, who in a few seconds had started to raise his hands as if to stop the man.

Then he was dead.

The men surrounding Igor gave no sign of having even heard the popping sound. Alice jerked, a small scream leaving her as Igor wrapped his hand tighter in her hair. Yanking her head back, leaving her with no option but to lean back into the man or fall.

Dominic saw red.

He drew his gun at his side. A little closer to one side and the motherfucking bastard was dead, but his father's hand stopped him.

"There is your compensation." The man was certifiably crazy. They were standing out in the open where anybody could see, and he had shot one of his men. And he was smiling about it.

Fucking crazy motherfucker, he thought.

"I'm not so sure this girl is going to be worth all this trouble. She must be good at sucking your cock, Dominic, no? Or maybe you, too, Sergio? Yes, why else all the trouble." He finished his words with a shake of his arm, sending Alice to her knees.

"Maybe I should test it."

Not even his father could hold him back this time as he leapt forward.

He didn't need to worry, though, because his father was right there alongside him as he raised his gun and started shooting. He might not have been raised to be a leader of the Familia, but he knew how to shoot. His father had made sure of it, and he used it now.

Shot after shot hit Igor's men square in the chest. Straight in the heart. They were dead before they hit the ground. There were bullets flying in all directions, from both sides, and he could hear Alice screaming.

All he focused on was the trigger.

Point, aim, pull.

Over and over.

His body took over as a feeling of anger so fierce came over him. Anger red-hot and burning. He let it take him as he kept the image of her on her knees in front of Igor. Threatening something so precious to him. You didn't threaten Familia. And right now, that was what he was.

His father grunted next to him. He didn't turn, but heard a guard drag him back to the vehicle for safety. Next was one of his father's guards. He was dead before he hit the ground.

Dominic managed to take two more of Igor's men down, shots to the chest. Danny took another one. There were only two left, and one was looking green around the edges. Dominic could see his hands shaking as he raised them in surrender, while Igor shouted to shoot them. He didn't have a care.

Another day Dominic would have taken the man's surrender.

Another day he would have shown mercy.

His father would have given him mercy and not killed him. But this was what made him different than his father. There wasn't any mercy. Not now. They had taken his woman. Stripped her, beaten her, and forced her to her knees.

No, today he wanted blood.

He wanted to watch as their blood spread across the ground, the life leaving all the men who had done him wrong.

He would take nothing else.

He raised his gun and fired, watching the bullet hit the man high on his chest. His shocked expression faded as he fell dead.

Danny took the last man, who managed to get off one more shot that clipped Dominic in the arm. He could feel the sting of the bullet, but he didn't stop. He kept his eyes on Alice.

Igor had let go of her hair in the shoot-out, taking several steps back, too intent on trying to protect himself. Leaving Alice unprotected but free as bullets flew around her.

She must not have noticed because she was still huddled on the ground, arms over her head. A position that his woman should never have been in.

Danny stopped standing behind him, watching, covering his back. Dominic kept going. Right up till he was standing inches from her, his eyes never leaving Igor.

"Alice." As he spoke she jerked up, her beautiful eyes flying to him. He didn't turn to look at her, though, keeping his eyes on his enemy.

His prey.

She sobbed and leapt up throwing her body into him. One of his arms came up to hold her to him, relief flooding him. It was the first moment of peace that he had felt in hours. That she was finally with him.

But she wasn't safe. Not yet. He didn't revel in his relief that she was there with him. He was too intent on the man in front of him.

245

His eyes never left Igor, who was watching Dominic with hatred in his eyes. He smirked and turned his head slightly toward her, kissing the side of her head. Knowing that it would enrage the man.

"Almost over; hang on to me, baby." Alice shuddered in his arms.

"You took her from me," Dominic stated, letting the man know exactly why he was going to kill him.

"You took her from me first! She was MINE!" Igor was losing it. His face was red and blotchy with anger, his body shaking with his rage.

Dominic smirked. For the first time in his life, he could see his father and grandfather in him.

Who he really was.

What he wanted was to take the man, chain him up, and torture him for days. Weeks. Never let him have the blessed sleep of death, but he couldn't. With Alice in his arms, he wanted her safe.

He needed it.

Besides, there was no better way for the man to die than for the last thing he saw to be her. Wrapped safe and lovingly in someone else's arms. His arms. To know that he had truly lost. That he would never have her because she was *his*.

"She's always been mine." His words were strong and final.

He fired, hitting the man first in one shoulder. Watching the shock and anger cross his features as he fired a second shot into the other shoulder.

The third hit his chest, low enough to not instantly kill him.

The fourth hit the man's groin and caused a squeal to leave Igor's already gaping mouth.

He smiled a sinister smile while watching Igor fall to his knees. Looking him straight in the eyes, letting him see the hatred burning within his own body.

The last bullet made its mark, perfect like a bullseye.

Dead center of his forehead.

Igor's body slid sideways and fell to the ground, dead.

Alice was shaking in his arms as he dropped the gun and wrapped both arms around her. His chest was heaving with the emotions running through it.

His revenge was complete.

"I've got you. I've got you, baby."

He would never let her go.

Chapter 38

Waking up in the hospital had been a relief for Alice. Dominic had been sleeping in the chair next to her, his head tilted sideways in a way that she wondered how bad his neck was going to be hurting later. She was lucky, though. Her injuries had been minor compared to everybody else's.

Dominic had just been grazed. When she had calmed down enough to actually notice his bloody arm, standing in the parking lot, waiting for some kind of cleanup crew, she had lost it.

The thought that he could have been hurt topped all the pain and fear that she had experienced over the last couple of days. She had been so distraught while the paramedics had worked on his arm that Danny had finally taken over and gotten her under control. It had been an easy fix, not even requiring stitches, and eventually she had settled down. The guilt, however, was still going strong.

Sergio was hit in the leg and would be just fine. He was headed back to the city to make sure that everything was good with Ivanov.

She had a hard time letting go of the fact that their clean break had been disrupted. None of them knew how long it would be before Sergio was free again. When he left, he told her that it was a minor sacrifice to see his son so happy with her and free. The guilt still ate at her.

Rick's injury had been more complicated. The bullet had struck him in the shoulder and caused lots of damage; she had been going to see him as often as she could. He told her that getting shot was nothing and that there wasn't much pain, but she knew that he was just doing it to put her at ease. She still worried.

Danny told her not to worry, saying, "The bastard is too tough to die now." Dominic had told her that he would look into physical therapy for him at the house so that he could come home.

Through all of the healing that everybody had to do, Dominic barely left her side. He said he was worried about her. The first night home she had slept like a baby. The stress of everything became too much for her and she had slept deep. It was the last night that she would sleep for a while.

It had now been a month. Rick was home, staying in one of the guest rooms while Danny stayed in another. Dominic had the gym downstairs configured so that Rick could do his physical therapy from there. For the most part, everyone had seemed to be okay.

However, they had still delayed their move for a few weeks, staying in Dominic's condo in the city at least until Rick was more stable.

Jason, the guard who had protected her and Taby, had also been okay. He had decided to stay with Sergio, not wanting to uproot his family, but had come by one evening to say goodbye. She had cried when he walked in with a limp. He had simply hugged her and told her that he was sorry he couldn't protect her.

Taby was okay. Although she had yet to see her, she had talked to her on the phone. She and Troy had decided to stay in the safehouse till she was better. She had a long road ahead of her, and her heart went out to her friend.

The guilt never wavered. It was constantly eating at her.

Two of Dominic's men had been killed. Taken from this life before their time. Taby and Troy's life had been ruined, and they would probably be scarred for life. All because of her. Because of her family.

Her real uncle had worked for the Western Crime Family, and that was where it had all started. Although her real uncle had never been a huge part of her life, it was weird to think that this all started when she was young.

Her uncle knew that his family was in danger due to who he was. So he had tried his best to keep them away. Safe and hidden under a fake name. She knew that he had probably been a good man in his own way.

After all, he had tried to hide his sister from his life, hoping to keep anything from touching them.

Little did he know that one man would start a circle that would forever alter everybody's world, with Igor's actions, killing her uncle and her parents it had set in motion a wave that would have ended horribly if it wasn't for that fateful night.

It was scary to think that if she hadn't gotten lucky that night, that if she hadn't escaped, her future would have been drastically different. There was no telling how she would have turned out.

She would have never met Dominic.

That was when the nightmares started to plague her. Visions of the horrors of what could have happened. That Dominic wasn't successful. She would always wake up drenched in sweat and screaming.

The first few times Dominic had woken with her and held her. After a few nights, though, she didn't want to wake him. So after he fell asleep, she would sneak out and sit on the floor by the window in the kitchen, looking out at the city lights.

That was what she was doing right now. Trying not to fall asleep for fear that the nightmares really would take over.

She knew that she needed to get some help. It was past the point of hoping that it would get better. Besides that, she was tired. She had even started to lose weight, and she knew that she had bags under her eyes.

"You know this isn't healthy." Dominic's voice in the otherwise quiet house made her jump.

"Gosh, you scared me!" She placed a hand over her thumping chest and smiled at him. She figured it came out weak when he didn't smile back or say anything. He stood there for the longest time.

"You know that this wasn't your fault, right?" he said, walking over and sitting by the window with her. Leave it to Dominic to know exactly what was going on in her head.

"Nobody would be hurt if it wasn't for me coming here. Taby would be free to live her life. It's all because of me." She sighed, the tiredness taking over her body. "The worst thing is that it could have been worse; you could have died." The last was said on a sob. He drew her into his arms and sat with her as she silently cried.

When she was mostly done, he stood, picking her up with him, and carried her back to their bed. Leaning against the headboard he wrapped his arms around her, pulling her into his body. Pulling up the covers, he got them settled in the bed before he started talking again.

"If I was to find someone for you to talk to, would you?" His voice was quiet, as if not wanting to break the silence after her crying jag.

"Like a therapist?" He nodded, and she thought about it. Could she talk to somebody else, a stranger?

"I won't force you, but I'm worried, sweetheart. You're not eating, you're not baking, you're not anything. Now you're not even sleeping." She went to interrupt him, and he shushed her.

"I know what you're doing, trying to make it so that you don't wake me. But if you think for one minute that I don't lie here all night long, wondering if you're okay, right up till you come back to bed, then baby, you are crazy. I love you. I know that it's hard to talk to me, and that's okay, but you have to talk to somebody. You have to get to the point where you can realize that none of this was your fault."

Tears leaked out of the corner of her eyes as he rolled her onto her back and came up on his elbows above her. Sheltering her, protecting her, always. That's how she felt with him. Why couldn't she talk to him?

"Baby … please," he whispered, worry in his eyes.

He placed one hand on her cheek, his thumb brushing away her tears.

It was the 'please' that did it.

This man was so strong he had never let her down, and she knew that he never would.

So, she started talking.

Long into the morning, she talked.

And like she knew he would, he took her pain and made it go away.

Leaving her protected, sheltered, and safe.

Always.

Chapter 39

When she woke it was to find that for once she wasn't alone in bed. She was wrapped around Dominic, her leg thrown over his hip. She knew he was awake, though, because his thumb was brushing against her shoulder.

She took a deep breath and realized that she felt refreshed. That she had slept peacefully. That it was gone. The crushing guilt. She was still sad, but it wasn't the overwhelming despair of guilt that she had been carrying around for days. Her beautiful man had given her that. For the first time in a month, she felt at peace.

She tilted her head up to look at him and found a heat so strong staring back at her. Fierce, searing desire that shot straight through her. They hadn't had sex since coming back. His injury had not allowed him, then his worry over her nightmares and just her in general.

Now that desire was like a cord pulled tight between them. A bond that would never be broken. His fingers slid through her hair to her neck, holding her in place as he rose enough to brush his lips against hers.

The littlest of contact not enough for him, and he flipped them easily. She felt him slide between her legs and drew them apart, making room for him as her hands wandered his strong back. Her t-shirt riding up at her waist, and bare from the waist down, she felt his skin against hers. He drew his nose along her throat as she arched up into him.

He sucked at her ear before he slid inside in one thrust.

Deep.

Beautiful.

Complete.

Epilogue

"Hey wake up, baby." Opening her eyes, she saw Dominic above her, frowning. She smiled up at him. He always got so worried.

"We landed." That made her sit up quickly.

"We did?" Excitement coursed through her.

In the last year, their life had had its ups and downs, but everybody had recovered physically and mentally. Rick was back to his normal moody self. He and Danny had bought a house not far from their own, making it easier to stay close to them.

Jason had done just fine. Sergio had even given him the recommendation that he needed to get in with the Ivanov. He was now working hard to become a lieutenant, and Sergio thought he would make it.

Sergio, of course, was off touring the world again. He came back every once in a while, with his new bride, but he was enjoying the peace. Just like they were.

Taby had taken some time. It wasn't until six months later that Alice would finally get to see her again. It was a heart-wrenching reunion. They had laughed and cried, and Taby had reassured her that she in no way blamed Alice. Telling her exactly what everybody else had.

She guessed that she'd just needed to hear it from Taby herself. It was a healing moment. Troy, although seeming relaxed, now clung to Taby a little tighter. Not that Taby seemed to mind. Their own story was long, and Alice figured after their ordeal, it was called for.

They had found a home on the coast of the Carolinas that Taby fell in love with. Alice had wanted them to come and live with them in Florida, but they were happy where they were. Besides, now that it was safe, they could very easily travel to see each other. She still missed her friend, though.

Her new home was wonderful. A nice house with a big screened-in front porch. She and Dominic often spent their nights out there, just taking in the peaceful life that they had worked so hard for. They had a view of rolling fields from their front porch. It always seemed to help calm them. To recenter them on what was important.

That they had made it out alive.

Eventually, they both had gone to see a therapist together. With Dominic's part in the whole ordeal, he also had trouble getting over what he had done and the fear of losing her.

It got to the point that, although they were talking with each other, they needed someone else, too. So, they had gone together. It had helped a lot, for both of them. It had also helped to bring them even closer.

That closer relationship had brought them to today. To taking a plane to a little town in Texas to where her parents had been buried. After she had found out about her real uncle, she had asked Dominic to find his body. She had thought that her mother would have liked to have known that her brother was at peace and buried with her.

Standing by their graves now, it also brought her a little peace. Knowing that her family had loved her with everything they had. Sacrificing everything for her. That they were now at peace.

She liked to think of her uncle as a loving man, that although he ran with a dangerous crowd, he had given up everything to keep his family safe. She would never forget his sacrifice.

"Hey." She heard a voice behind her and turned in Dominic's arms to see Taby and Troy. She gasped and rushed forward, wrapping her arms around her friend.

"You look so good! And your hair! You went blond!" she said as she drew back to get a good look at her.

"Hey, Troy!" she said enthusiastically.

"Hey girl," he said with a slightly twisted smile, showing his humor for the two girls in front of him.

"What are you doing here?"

"We wouldn't miss this for anything," Taby said cryptically.

"Miss what?" Alice asked, puzzled.

"Turn around and see."

Turning around with a smile on her face, she saw that Dominic was no longer standing, but kneeling right behind her, and in his hand was a black jewelry box with a sparkling ring inside.

Too shocked, she stood there staring at him, her heart in her throat.

Was he really going to ask her?

She slowly walked forward till she was standing in front of him.

"Alice Beckman, I know that this may be a weird spot for some." She heard Taby giggle behind her.

"But for us, I couldn't think of a better spot than in front of our friends and family than to ask you to marry me."

She saw two men walk up beside her and realized it was Danny and Rick. Everybody she loved was here. Tears ran down her face, barely able to speak, her emotions so strong, powerful, and beautiful. The feeling of safety and love that were always there because of him, and all she could do was whisper one word.

"Yes.

Playlist

'I Found You' by Andy Grammar

'Put Me In My Place' by Muscadine Bloodline

'Cover Me Up' by Morgan Wallen

'Go Fuck Yourself' by Two Feet

'Say' by Ruel

'You Are the Reason' by Calum Scott

'Dazed and Confused' by Ruel

'I Lived' by OneRepublic

'Everything I Want' by Billie Eilish

• K.B. Barrett • Everything I Need •

Thank You

I would like to say thank you to my husband.

Thank you for supporting me. Without you, this would never have been possible. You are my Happily Ever After.

Thank you to my friends who answered my never-ending list of questions. You might not know it, but you helped me fulfill a dream.

To my editor. Thank you for all your help in making Everything I Need live up to it's potential. I wouldn't be here without you.

K.B Barrett lives in western Michigan with her wonderful husband and three kids. Her love of books started early, due to her grandmother who was an avid reader and encouraged her to love all books.

Eventually, she had too many ideas and so she started writing her own books. She loves camping with her husband, traveling to new destinations, and enjoying coffee in one of her many colorful mugs.

KB Barrett

www.authorkbbarrett.com